THE
ADVENTURES OF
GUM

BUMMER SUMMER

*Lucy —
Get ready to
laugh out loud!
Best Wishes —
Lucie Brouther*

THE
ADVENTURES OF
GUM

BUMMER SUMMER

JULIE BROTHERS

LifeRich
PUBLISHING
an imprint of The Reader's Digest Association, Inc.

LifeRich Publishing books may be ordered
through booksellers or by contacting:

LifeRich Publishing
1663 Liberty Drive
Bloomington, IN 47403
www.liferichpublishing.com
1 (888) 238-8637

ISBN: 978-1-4897-0053-7 (sc)
ISBN: 978-1-4897-0055-1 (hc)
ISBN: 978-1-4897-0054-4 (e)

Library of Congress Control Number: 2013919714

Printed in the United States of America.

LifeRich Publishing rev. date: 01/30/2014

To Mom, Dad, and Big John

Your love lives forever!

*"It ain't what you don't know
that gets you into trouble.
It's what you know for sure
that just ain't so."*
—MARK TWAIN

Contents

Preface

To the Reader,

Gum is always in my life! It seems like my son, Jake, chews gum all of the time. After school, you will find him roaming the halls trying to "bum" a piece of gum. The supermarket visit isn't complete until he picks out some strange pack of gum at the checkout counter. The candy store at the mall is his very favorite place. He takes his time and is careful about his gum selection. One day I told him that his nickname should be "Gum" since he chews so much gum. This was just a nickname between us, until now!

Gum has inspired me to share his love of gum by creating a character that is a mixture of us both. I hope you enjoy *The Adventures of Gum: Bummer Summer* and that Gum not only becomes a new friend, but I also hope you see a little bit of yourself in this new character as you explore the contents of this book.

GUM is waiting on YOU!

Acknowledgment

I would like to acknowledge my wonderful family who was patient and kind as I spent many hours writing. My husband, John, you are the reason I wake up in the morning and tackle life as it hits me head on. Thank you for believing in me and helping me achieve all of my many dreams. Thank you to my son, Jake, for letting me live my childhood again through your eyes and for just being a cool kid who loves gum! Jonita, thank you for pushing me to write and bothering me until I finally did it. To J.R., Angela, and Easton, thanks for the humor and fun times on the farm. You should charge admission! To Mi Mi and Papa, thanks for providing my son with adventures of his own while I worked on the book.

Special thanks go out to all of the kids on the 1-1-5 for never failing to provide our street with humor and character. Each of you makes this street a great place to live. To all of the kids I have taught over the years, thanks for the stories and laughs. I, by far have been the one blessed! Thanks to Mills Elementary for helping me keep my head above water this past year. You are the most amazing co-workers! To my editing team (Cherie, Dana, Dawn, Kara, and Terry) you are the best and the brightest! Thanks for the extra sets of eyes!

ntroduction

Meet Gum, a kid that enjoys his summers off. Gum seizes every opportunity and makes the most out of life, or should I say "adventure". Living on the edge and having fun seem to be what he thinks about most. That is until his teacher, Mrs. Magle, destroys everything and messes up his entire summer with one "special announcement". How will Gum survive this terrible turn of events? How will he distract his mother? Adventure and excitement, that's how!

Prologue

School gets in the way of everything! Don't get me wrong, I understand there are things to learn. I just wish it didn't take so long. There are several questions I have and it would be nice if a grown up would answer them. For instance, have you ever wondered why we only get two days off a week, and why it's called a "weekend"? Who decided to throw this off balance with five school days and two days off? Why can't we chew gum at school if we agree to sign a contract stating "I will not stick my gum to my desk"?

I'm not really the "speak up" type, but if I were on the student council I'd push to get gum legal again. I'm sure the "reasons" we can't chew gum have left by now. There would be less talking in class if everyone could chew gum. Teachers might like it if they try it. The other day the principal came over the speaker and said that there is no gum chewing allowed at school and for the person who brought the blue bubble gum to please stop. I heard that the bus driver on bus 41 allows you to chew bubble gum. She even gives you gum when you get on the bus. I wish I rode the bus!

I ride to school with my mom every day. Yep, she's a teacher. She never leaves my side! Imagine getting sent to school with your mom every day. Imagine your mom always being one step ahead of your every move. I have tried to plead my case with my dad, but he always tells me to quit complaining. I like her, but I don't want to go to school with her every day. Do you go to school with your mom every day? GEEZ, can a kid catch some slack every now and then?

Chapter One

Gum, Da-Dum-Dum...DUM!

Dear Summer,

Where have you been? I've waited on you for 280 days! I chew three pieces of gum a day to pass the time, so that is 840 pieces of gum. Tomorrow is the first day of summer break and I am so ready to take advantage of all you have to offer. Right now I am sitting in class on the last day of school. I'm certain that my teacher has no other plans for the day. She told us to write in our journals and keep notes about our last day of school. She even told us to journal our feelings about summer. Who journals about their "feelings"? BLAH! This is going

to be a long day. This may be the longest day I have ever endured in the fourth grade! Mrs. Magle says we should become "one" with our writer's notebooks. That seems like an impossible task! I am human and you are a notebook. I do not understand why teachers do this to kids. I like to write stories about space ships, sword fighting, and my dog Lizzy. I also like to write stories about gum. I love gum! Gum is good. Gum stays with you until you get rid of it and sometimes you find it in the strangest places like on your shoe, a rollercoaster seat, on the sidewalk, under the table, or even stuck to the bathroom wall. You can even make gum. Gum is great! Spending the last day of school journal writing is NOT.

I want to talk to my friends. I want to ask Matthew if he plans to meet me at the neighborhood park after school to try out our new fishing net. Yesterday we caught a frog. I tried to get it to chew a piece of gum, but it wouldn't. Maybe it didn't like the flavor, I'm not sure. That may be something we need to check out later. Right now I am stuck writing. I am supposed to be writing about our last day of fourth grade, and I can't keep my mind off of summer. It's just right around the corner. I feel like a hungry person staring at a big piece of steak! My mind can't think about anything else. Well, almost anything else. I think about gum a lot. I think about gum so much that my mom, dad, and friends call me Gum. My mother says I have an "unhealthy obsession" with gum. Most people wake up and think about what they will have for breakfast or what they will wear. Not me, nope! I think about what kind of gum I'll chew. There are

so many flavors! The choices are difficult, but I manage. That's another thing that makes today so hard. There is NO GUM CHEWING at school. Tomorrow I get to begin my gum chewing marathon once again. One time we made gum in class, but the teacher said we couldn't chew it because it was against school policy. Who makes gum and doesn't chew it? I took it home and savored the fine flavor of Root Beer gum.

I should probably tell you my name in case anyone picks up this masterpiece diary and wants to read about what I think, yeah right! My name is Jake, but I rarely use that name. I only use the name at awards assemblies, the dentist's office, and at church. Mom said that there are certain places nicknames shouldn't be used. I like the name Gum. It describes me well. I should probably go now. My teacher said we should finish our last thought because it's time to go to gym class. I sure hope my gym teacher doesn't make us journal. I need to move around.

Dear Summer,

I am back. Gym class was fun. Mrs. Magle told us to take our seats and journal about gym. She really didn't plan for the last day of school. She is running around the classroom with her checklist unplugging cables, wrapping computers with trash bags, and cleaning off her desk. She said she had some great news to share

with us later, but we had to keep writing and if everyone followed directions, we would get to hear the exciting news. Maybe she is going to tell us that we get to chew gum after lunch. Maybe she found out a way to make summers last longer. I better keep writing.

We used the spring launcher to jump over a beam in gym, and that was a lot of fun. I flung through the air like Jimmy Fitznally's meatball in the cafeteria yesterday. Jimmy's mom never packs his lunch. He hates the cafeteria food, so he gets in trouble in the cafeteria and then his mom has to send his lunch for detention the next day. My mom doesn't like Jimmy as much as my other friends. She said he does nothing but encourages bad news. My mom is a teacher at my school. She teaches across the hall from my classroom. That's another reason I am writing and following directions. My mom has this special teacher sensor topped off with a super-duper mom radar. She can have her classroom door shut and sense when I am not following directions. One time I was picking off the tips of the glue bottles to collect them and my mom walked in and gave me that half-mom, half-teacher stare and walked out. Even my teacher didn't see me! It's freaky. She can sense when my dad is about to do something crazy too.

I REALLY think my teacher is going to tell us something big! She keeps smiling at us every time she checks something off of her list. We definitely get to chew gum in class TODAY. I am about to burst into flames! Holding the anticipation inside is like shaking a pop bottle and expecting nothing to happen. What

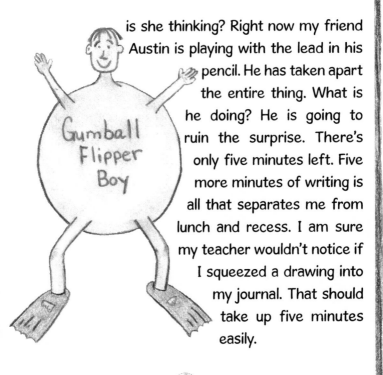

Gumball
Flipper
Boy

is she thinking? Right now my friend Austin is playing with the lead in his pencil. He has taken apart the entire thing. What is he doing? He is going to ruin the surprise. There's only five minutes left. Five more minutes of writing is all that separates me from lunch and recess. I am sure my teacher wouldn't notice if I squeezed a drawing into my journal. That should take up five minutes easily.

Dear Summer,

This surprise is really big. We just got back from recess, and my teacher is super happy. She is "more than usual" happy. She waited at the door for us and called each of us by name. I don't smell gum, but this news has to be good. She told us to write about recess. Here it goes...I played. May in Oklahoma is HOT! Some days we have to play inside because the heat index is over 100 degrees. Once Mrs. Magle took us outside and we tried the fried egg experiment on a sheet of aluminum foil.

It worked! And again, we couldn't eat it. She said we aren't supposed to eat science. I was well prepared to get sick and would have tried it. Once a kid brought dry ice and a water bottle for science class, and we had to go outside for the demonstration. Mrs. Magle closed the container and made us all get away so we wouldn't get hurt. What she didn't realize was it went off right outside the first grade classroom window. Boy, were those kids scared! We ran back into the classroom and she called the office to let them know that everyone was okay. I love it when we do science. Mrs. Magle allows us to pick whatever science project we want, and we get to be the scientists. That's fun! I wish we were doing science right now.

Mrs. Magle is calling us in a circle on the floor. I think she's about to tell us about the awesome news. Maybe we get out of school early. SUMMER, I LOVE YOU!

Dear Not-So-Swell Summer,

What a bummer! I can't believe this. Mrs. Magle just gave us the "wonderful news". She spoke with the principal yesterday and there's a fifth grade teaching spot available. She is going to teach fifth grade next year. She asked the principal and the counselor to keep her entire class together for fifth grade and that's the news! We waited all this time only to be told that we

were going to be in her class next year too. She sure isn't good at planning surprises. I asked her if we were going to get to chew gum and she said no. A guy can always dream, can't he?

That wasn't all the news. This day just keeps getting worse! Mrs. Magle said that since she'll be our teacher next year, she's going to send home a letter to our parents along with our writer notebooks. She said we needed to journal at least three times per week over the summer. Did you hear me? OVER THE SUMMER is the worst news I could have received. I may barf! I feel sick! I might just throw myself to the zombies. I wonder if it is okay to pray for a zombie apocalypse. That wouldn't be so bad. What am I going to do? I thought about hiding it, but Mrs. Magle sends emails to all the parents about everything that goes on at school. I think that's why my mom likes my teacher so much. THIS IS AWFUL! What could be worse? I have written all day. Mrs. Magle dismissed us from the circle and told us to write about our "feelings". I hope she doesn't read this because I feel ruined, betrayed, left in the cold, and sucker punched all at the same time! What a bummer summer this will be!

I hate this news. I hate

this news. I hate this news.

Okay, I'm sure you understand I hate this news! I like my teacher, but assigning a writing assignment for the summer is just plain wrong. What will I write about?

Summer journaling + Psycho Teacher Mom =
Disaster Summer

My mom just popped over into my classroom and gave my teacher thumbs up. She asked the class if we heard the good news yet. She even came over and hugged me (in class) and said she was so excited. Mrs. Magle told her she had more good news. In front of the class, she told my mom that we get to take home our writing notebooks and write all summer long. My mom jumped up and down AND clapped her hands. She is crazy, mad, AND insane! This has made her day. She has been launched into eternal happiness. She will plan a summer learning schedule and writing will be part of the

schedule. My mom doesn't do what is asked. She doubles it! If my teacher says read 20 minutes, I pull double duty and read 40 minutes. She thinks working me harder will somehow pay off. Dad never says a word. He just says, "Son, listen to your mother!" I am all alone on this one. BOOM! CRASH! THUD!

THIS STINKS!

Chapter Two

Nazi Mom Ruins Summer

Dear Bummer Summer,

Today is the first day of my BUMMER SUMMER! Mom made "our" schedule last night. I thought for sure she would take a day off and let us coast into the summer, but noooooooo! She said she didn't want me getting "accustomed to the foolishness" summer has to offer. Foolishness? She is MENTAL! Dad needs to have her committed. My mom wasn't always a teacher. She taught when she graduated from college and then moved on to work at a college. Apparently, I made the mistake

and acted like I missed her bunches when I was three and she flipped and started teaching again. Who would have known that at three years old I'd destroyed my own future? I pulled her to this moment. If she was still working at the college, I'd be home alone like all the other kids. Instead, I have Super-Nazi-Kill-Your-Summer Mom who has sunken her teeth into my entire summer. OH WAIT! This gets worse. My mom is best friends with Mrs. Magle. She's going to have extra motivation!

Top Ten Things I'd Rather Do Than Write All Summer Long:

1. I'd rather eat a million worms covered in fish guts.
2. I'd rather lick the bottom of Jimmy Fitznally's shoe that he used to squash a spider.
3. I'd rather pick up dog poo.
4. I'd rather jump off of the Empire State Building.
5. I'd rather eat the cafeteria beef and noodle surprise all summer long.
6. I'd rather get sucked up by a tornado and fly through the universe.
7. I'd rather mow every lawn in the neighborhood.
8. I'd rather organize our local library and shelve books (maybe not).
9. I'd rather babysit my neighbor's crazy dog that has seizures and barfs up everything he eats.
10. I'd rather go to school in my underwear ON THE FIRST DAY BACK!

Okay, she just got out the timer and patted me on the back. She said I should probably write for about 20 minutes a day so I can "clean out my creative pipes". Really? Creative pipes? I think she's gone overboard. I'm not sure what planet she's from. Maybe she's from one of those places they haven't explored yet. I wish the President hadn't shut down most of NASA because they could've helped us return her back to her original planet. I'm certain she has tentacles somewhere. That may be why she can sense it when I'm not on track in class. That's it! SHE IS AN ALIEN! Oh no, it's even worse to have a Nazi-Alien Mom. That could explain why Dad always says, "Do what your mother says, son." She took over his brain too. He fell in love with an alien! The FBI should know about this. I should really inform them that there is extraterrestrial life here in Oklahoma. People think Oklahoma is a quiet place, but we have aliens! There has to be more. I'll start a club!

FBI LOG TOP SECRET

Dear Bummer Summer,

My summer writing journal has now turned into an FBI log. My mom is an alien. I'm sure I've been taken hostage by an alien. She's captured my dad and has taken over his mind also. Right now the Nazi-Alien Mom has started the timer and has me writing for 20 minutes. I don't think this is a writing assignment at all. I think she's making me write in order to obtain my thoughts and take over my brain. This explains it all! Mrs. Magle has to be an alien too! Mrs. Magle has manipulated the school principal and has the entire class writing all summer so they can learn more about humans. No other teacher has done this to their class. I checked! All of the other kids have been given freedom this summer. This explains EVERYTHING! Okay, keep calm! I CAN'T KEEP CALM. I HAVE AN ALIEN WATCHING MY EVERY MOVE! I will counteract and write about HER every move. Then when she goes in for the kill, I'll have documentation to leave behind for the FBI.

Right now she's making salsa. I'm sitting at the kitchen table, and she's in the kitchen making salsa. Who makes salsa? It's in every grocery store. We love salsa, especially her salsa! I wonder if she puts some sort of microchip into the salsa which enables her to track information about how our bodies work. Maybe she uploads it to her iPad and sends it to Roswell, New Mexico. I did a report on Area 51 in school and she was able to help me more

than any other person. She seemed to know a lot about aliens. She knew stories that I could not find in any book. It's hard though to stay away from the salsa. How do I keep Dad from eating the salsa? He's pacing in the kitchen. Oh no, he's going for a chip! Going, going, GONE! Dad has just consumed radioactive alien solution. He isn't stopping! He's going crazy! Goodness dude, STOP! I can't interrupt my research and stop him. Mom would for sure know that something was up. She's very smart and can think faster than any of us. Note to self: Stay away from the salsa! Bummer Summer, I have to go now. My 20 minutes is up!

Bummer Summer,

I got on the Internet and searched "Alien Moms" and "How to Report an Alien". Nothing I could use showed up in the search. Next, I searched "How to Report Extraterrestrials". That helped. I am getting closer to getting this alien out of my house. Dad and I will be happier. I'll be able to continue with my summer without writing in this notebook. I started a club yesterday. Jimmy thinks my mom is an alien also. We went up and down the street and recruited members for the club. So far, I have Jimmy, Erin, Matthew, Rachel, Catie, Maddie, Sam, Logan, Molly, and Palmer. Sam, Molly, Palmer, and Logan are really young, so I'm not sure they understand.

Sam was wearing a superman cape when he signed our sheet and was running around in circles screaming that he was going to save the world. After he signed, he started screaming he was going to save the world from alien moms. Now that I think about it, he might be an alien child. Logan just scribbled his name. Palmer said, "Let's do it!", and Molly asked to see my dog. We may have to keep them at a distance. We don't need anyone messing this up!

Erin is going to research how to report an alien to the FBI. Matthew is going to use binoculars to keep an eye on Mrs. Magle. Rachel is going to interview my mom about aliens to ask more questions. Catie is going to ask her mom how you keep aliens out of your head since she is a nurse. Maddie said she's going to make up a cheer so she can celebrate when the mission is accomplished. Jimmy and I are going to keep watching my mom and will probably try to pick out the best gum to chew for our next meeting. I'm thinking watermelon since it's summer, but Jimmy thinks we should chew plain bubble gum so we can keep focused. The others didn't get jobs assigned to them. They are "on call" in case we need them.

Dear Bummer Summer,

Operation Nazi-Alien Mom is coming together. This isn't one of my 20 minute writings. I just wanted to tell you

that the plan is moving forward. I also wanted to note my actions should the FBI need documentation regarding this master plan.

Dear Bummer Summer,

Erin gave me the information she saw online to report extraterrestrial activity. Step number one tells us to call local law enforcement. THE POLICE? What if they upset her? How will she react? Are they going to believe me? The information Erin gave me also says we should stay calm. How am I supposed to stay calm when I live in the same house with an alien?

Dear Bummer Summer,

My alien Mom took me to the mall in Tulsa. I think she suspects something is going on. She told me I could go to the Mega Candy Shop and buy an entire pound of bubble gum. I made my selections carefully and took about 45 minutes to fill my bag. For an alien, she was very patient and didn't seem to mind that I was taking my sweet time. I told her I felt like a kid in a candy store and she reminded me that I was a kid in the candy store.

I know for sure now that she's an alien. She walked the entire mall twice and only bought one item. What Mom can walk the entire mall twice and only buy one item? None, that's how many! She even sat at one of those center booths and let someone half way curl her hair. No mom does that! If you buy the curling iron they finish your hair, but not my mom. She got up and told the guy doing the demonstration she would "think about it". Maybe she's making a list of all the things she needs to take back with her when she returns to her planet. Even worse, maybe she's making a list of all the things she shouldn't destroy when all of the other aliens come to take over our planet! Oh man! This is going to get nasty!

The candy thing threw me off a bit, but I think that's exactly what she wanted. She knows I'm up to something. Tomorrow is the big day. Tomorrow, our club will meet and we will call the police. She better be ready. After tomorrow, the police will come get her, lock her up in a lab somewhere, and there'll be NO MORE SUMMER WRITING! I'll play ALL DAY and my summer will officially start. Woo Hoo!

Dear REALLY Bummer Summer,

Calling the police on your mom isn't such a great idea. I'm in trouble right now, but will write later. I have a lot to tell you. This is bad! Really bad! I may not make it out alive.

Dear Deadly Summer,

I feel it is important that I leave a written record of my wishes.

To my dad, I leave my baseball card collection. You can even have my autographed baseballs.

To my cousin Easton, I leave my coin collection left to me by Papa Alfred and my skateboard.

To Matthew, I leave my LEGO collection and all building materials.

To Jimmy, I leave my gum sculpture. It took a while to make it, so don't leave it in the sun.

To my mom, I leave my drawing set. I didn't mean to hurt you. I really thought you were an alien.

To my Grandma Jo, I leave my collection of watches. I enjoyed finding them with you.

To my Papa Jerry, I leave my toy car collection. I enjoyed our recent trip to Branson.

To my MiMi, I leave you my swim flippers and scuba goggles.

To my cousin Angela, I leave you my roll of duct tape. I am not sure what all you can do with it, but the girls in the neighborhood sure seem crazy about making things with duct tape.

To my dog Lizzy, I leave you all of my stuffed animals. You can chew the eyes out of them all. That's okay! Just enjoy them, because I'm certain that after tonight, I'll be **dead meat!**

Dear Sad and Lonely Bummer Summer,

I'm just not sure where things took such a turn towards Doom Street. One minute I'm sitting in class waiting for summer to start, and the next thing I know I'm in solitary confinement for a crime that mom says was family treason. I looked up the word treason in my online dictionary and it means "betrayal of trust or confidence". That seems to be pushing the situation a bit too far. Apparently, my mother isn't an alien life form, but how was I supposed to know?

I've learned that you shouldn't create a club made up of kids in a neighborhood where an investigation is taking place. Parents talk! Erin printed two copies of "How to Report Extraterrestrial Activity" off of the Internet and her mom noticed the copy. She asked Erin a lot of questions and apparently Erin's mom is really good at detective work like my mom, because Erin spilled the beans. She told her mom everything.

To make things worse, Matthew was caught looking into Mrs. Magle's living room window with binoculars. She got scared and called the police. Matthew's parents had to convince the police to not take him to the big house! He was forced to tell them what was going on and my name (of course) was mentioned. Matthew was forced into unloading our plan to the police in exchange for his

freedom. I don't blame him; I wouldn't want to go to the slammer either.

Rachel didn't get a chance to interview my mom about aliens, but Catie did ask her mom how to keep aliens out of your head. Jimmy was able to stay disconnected from the situation. He didn't get in any trouble. His mom works a lot so he didn't have anyone home when the police showed up to capture Matthew a.k.a. "the peeper".

It was bad, the police showed up to my door with Matthew and his parents. The police immediately asked to speak to my mom. Instead, I stepped outside thinking we could handle this and told them I thought my mom was an alien and would do something terrible to them like laser beam their heads off if they confronted her. They didn't believe me! Mom must have "sensed" that I was outside talking to someone because she just appeared. (I still find that strange!) She asked the police what was going on and Matthew's parents busted us. They coughed up the plan about our club, turning my mom into the police, spying on Mrs. Magle, and the whole nine yards. Erin's mom was watering her flowers and came over when she saw the police in the yard. I saw a nightmare unfold before my eyes. My life was being dismantled and overrun with terror. I didn't think I would make it out of the situation alive. I was going down in flames while everyone else stepped outside of the smoke to watch.

Of course my mom was furious. She apologized to the police, to Matthew's parents, and to Erin's mom. She even walked me over to Mrs. Magle's house and made me sit down and explain the whole situation to my teacher. How

EMBARRASING! My mom told the police that I was an adventurer whose mind "goes a little crazy" every once in a while and that she promised I would get checked out by a psychologist to ensure I didn't have voices in my head telling me to follow through with these silly ideas. The police officers smiled at me and patted me on the back. One even whispered to me, "I think you'll be one busy little boy this summer!" How dare he? All I wanted was to be rid of my alien mother. How was I supposed to know she wasn't an alien? Mom always says that in our house you are guilty until proven innocent.

Mrs. Magle was surprised to see us. She thought we were just stopping by for a visit. My mom told her that my imagination had gone too far this time and that I needed to explain what I'd been up to so far this summer. We are just a week into summer and I'm already asking for forgiveness for my sins and not only that, I've been taken to my teacher's house for final judgment. Oh boy! I explained the situation to my teacher. She laughed, assured me she wasn't an alien and told me that the writer's notebook was simply a way for me to channel my imagination and creativity. REALLY? Seems I have enough imagination and creativity to go around the whole neighborhood. Mom assured Mrs. Magle that I'd be doing lots of "channeling" this summer. I know what that means. It only means that the summer teacher stuff is going to get a lot harder. At this point, I'm a victim of my own creation.

I walked away from Mrs. Magle's house feeling as though I'd buried myself six feet under. There was no way

to recover from the police lighting up your neighborhood. As we walked back to our house, all eyes were on us. Everyone was outside. Dad had even made his way out and was visiting with Matthew's dad. As if being stared down by neighborhood eyes wasn't enough, my mom GRABBED MY HAND! Yes, she put her hand in mine and held my hand! I don't know if she thought she was giving me courage to get to the house or was trying to ruin my reputation or what. I was in no position to remove my hand. I feared what might happen if I jerked away from her display of public affection at a time like this. PDA with your mom? GROSS! I was an elephant in the room the size of a closet. The world couldn't get any smaller! All eyes were on me. My spine was burning and everyone was watching the flame behind my back. I closed my eyes and held on to my mom's hand. She walked me to the door and told me to stay inside. Then, she went in for the kill. She told me "not to worry about anything" and that we would "talk about it later"! Don't worry? REALLY? Worrying is all I can think about. It's a natural state at a time like this. Get in trouble, worry, and wait for your punishment. That's how things are supposed to go. It is the natural order. See, this is what I meant by my mom being smart. She knows just what to say to make you not hate her. You end up feeling bad and dysfunctional. She should lock me in the cellar and throw away the key. She should tell me to prepare to meet my maker. But not my mom, my mom holds my hand, walks me to the door, and tells me not to worry about it. I'm sure she was trained to torture kids.

My parents are masters when it comes to making you feel bad about the things you have done. Mom and Dad stayed outside for a really long time. I could hear them laughing. They were really having fun. Are they laughing at me? Is the whole neighborhood out there recounting my recent imaginative combustion? How will I ever be able to walk out in my yard again? Fishing at the ponds won't seem right. Swimming in our neighborhood pool will be embarrassing. Forget playing at the park. Oh well, pretty sure after my parents get done with me I'll be listed as missing on all the local news channels. Good-bye summer! I sure didn't want to spend my entire vacation writing to you, but I never would've imagined that our relationship would end this way. I think I kind of enjoyed it while it lasted. You really weren't so bad.

Dear Not So Deadly Summer,

I was not tortured and killed as recently predicted. My life expectancy has been extended to include the next few weeks assuming I don't find myself in more trouble. Mom and Dad are making me go the entire night without talking about the incident. When they got in, I told them I was sorry and it wouldn't happen again. Mom and Dad exchanged glances as some sort of top secret communication and Mom said we shouldn't talk about things now and we would talk about them later. I

wish they would just punish me and get it over with! This is TORTURE! Waiting this long should be illegal. There should be a kid court where you can receive punishment and a judge makes sure that you don't get beaten. I could sure use a judge right now. Maybe I should look on the Internet for a kid judge. How would I pay them? It seems that they have to take payment in other forms besides money if they are working to represent kids. I do have almost a pound of bubble gum and that is sure to entice anyone on a bench.

Dear Lonely Summer,

Parents make no sense. I have stayed up all night long thinking about what form of punishment would be coming my way. I am staying in my room and out of the line of fire. No one has checked in on me. No one has yelled at me. No one is saying a word to me. Mom didn't even sit me down with a timer and tell me to write. I'm being left alone. Now, I'm really scared! Maybe they are making arrangements to sell me to another country for child labor. I should start packing my bag.

Things to Pack Before Getting Sold Into Child Labor:

1. Gum
2. A good pair of walking shoes
3. Underwear

4. My Retainers

5. Beef Jerky

6. My Kindle

7. Hat

8. Some Legos

9. Water Bottle

10. Writer's Notebook—This is only for documentation in case I go missing!

Dear Summer,

Things are looking up. It looks like I won't be sold into child labor. I think it is safe to unpack my bag. Mom and Dad came in as a unified team and sat on both sides of me while I was playing on my bed. At first, I thought they were going to tie me up and ship me off in a box with breathing holes across the ocean, but they didn't have any restraints in their hands. Mom said she wasn't mad, she was just a little surprised that I would mistake her for an alien. She said she loved me no matter what and I was her kid through thick and thin. Dad said he thinks Mom is an alien sometimes too, but it's always best to do what Mom says. It does make life easier and now I know exactly what it means. I wonder if he has tried to turn her in to the FBI. He seemed to be speaking from experience.

They went on to tell me it's okay to make mistakes. Apparently before Nana passed away last year, Nana told Momma that I needed to be allowed to make more mistakes. She said that mistakes are opportunities to learn and that kids have a lot of learning to do. I guess you can say that Nana knew I'd be in BIG trouble someday. So if you can hear me Nana, Thanks!

Chapter Three

Boat Voyage!

Dear Summer,

My Nana passed away from cancer last year, and then Papa had a heart attack and went to meet Nana in heaven. Since then, we visit the farm where my Nana and Papa lived. It's the same farm where my mom and uncle grew up. Mom says we have a lot of work to do. Dad can't go since he works during the summer, but Mom says we need to go get the place cleaned up. Tomorrow we head out for the farm. We won't stay at Nana and Papa's farm because it makes Mom sad, but we'll get to stay at my Uncle Melvin and Aunt Jamie's farm. This only means that I get to spend more time with my cousin

Easton. I can't wait! An entire week on the farm! I have to be prepared for whatever awaits us on the farm. I need to make this entry short so I can go pack my Wal-Mart sacks. For some reason, Mom never uses luggage to go to the farm. Everything gets packed in Wal-Mart sacks. Everyone gets two sacks. I'm not sure why. We have really nice luggage!

Dear Summer,

We are loaded in the truck and are on our way to the farm. (We take Dad's truck because Mom doesn't like taking the car down the country roads.) Mom says I need to leave my video games at home. She said that after the most recent turn of events, I'm in need of fresh air and lots of sunshine. I kind of agree, although I was looking forward to showing Easton how far I made it through Turbo Alien Blaster II. She did say I could bring my writer's notebook. It isn't a game, but I guess it will do. At this point, I'm in no position to argue. I need to be on good behavior because I heard Mom and Dad talk about our vacation surprise later this summer. I don't want to miss out and they'll leave me behind. My parents take vacations seriously. Dad likes to take vacation self-portraits. Last year he almost fell into the Grand Canyon. Mom started screaming and all the tourists were watching. I just pretended I was with another family. They make friends with everyone too. I

bet my parents have met more people on vacations than in our own neighborhood. They are sort of "out there" and I don't understand them sometimes.

The farm makes my mom sad. As we got closer, Mom stopped the car and started crying. I asked her if it would be okay to be there and she said she'd be fine. I don't think she's going to be fine. She seems sad. Not in an alien sort of way either. She seems very sad in a way that I would be if something happened to my parents. I can't imagine not having my mom and dad. I need to go help my mom. We are here. Time to unpack for cousin camp!

Dear HOT Summer,

Mom seems better. She spent the day cleaning up the house, and I spent the day playing with my cousin Easton. Aunt Jamie is a teacher too, so they came over to Nana and Papa's farm to help. I don't think Easton and I are much help though. We went outside to explore. Papa has some strange things lying around the farm. We figured we needed to build a fort since we'd be here a lot this summer. We decided we should use an old boat out in the pasture. It's yellow and creaks when you step into it. I'm sure there are other things living in it, but when you step out for an adventure like this, you have to be willing to accept whatever comes your way. That includes nature!

We started by cleaning out all the old tree limbs that had fallen into the boat from the big storm last week. There was also some grass that had grown up in the boat, so we pulled it out. Mom said it made her nervous that we were playing in the boat, but I guess it didn't make her too nervous, because she brought us sheets and blankets and helped us carry Nana's old rugs to the boat to help cover the holes in the boat bottom. Mom said she and Uncle Melvin used to do this sort of thing all of the time. I can't imagine my mom having fun like this. I wonder if she used to make Uncle Melvin a schedule every summer.

Tonight we are tired. Tomorrow Uncle Melvin promised us a campfire. We can't wait! Mom said we can stay up a little bit planning our new fort, but we are super tired. Oklahoma heat just zaps the juice right out of a person. Half way through today, Easton suggested we turn the boat into a swimming boat, but I told him we would have too many holes in the boat and the water would for sure leak out.

Dear Not-So-Bad Summer,

Sleeping on a farm is a lot different than sleeping in town. On the farm, I wake up early because of all the country sounds. My dad was right. It sounds like every animal is trying to wake you up. Outside my bedroom window

is a big turkey. Her name is Kevin. I don't understand why they named a girl turkey "Kevin". Seems odd, but that's her name. She likes shiny metal things so she keeps pecking at the window trying to get to Easton's model cars. She won't stop. She keeps pecking as if she expects the window to break through at any time. I don't know how everyone else can sleep through these sounds. Earlier I heard the sound of a rooster. He started crowing really early. I tried to keep sleeping, but I found myself hoping to figure out what it was he was trying to say. Papa Alfred would say he's just earning a paycheck, but I never believed roosters earned paychecks. How would they cash them? Mom grew up on a farm. She told me they are letting the other roosters know they are claiming territory and sometimes they crow to let the hens and chicks know about potential predators. Either way, I'm glad I'm not a rooster. They never stop. I wouldn't want to be the reason people couldn't sleep. Maybe today Aunt Jamie will let us help gather eggs.

My uncle's farm is full of animals. There is a donkey named Jack. He lets you ride him. Jack is funny because he scratches his bottom on the fence. It always looks like he's trying to sit on the fence. Jack loves apples and sugar cubes. Maybe we'll get to feed Jack this afternoon. My Papa's dog is there too. Rudy is a trick dog. When Easton and I were smaller, Papa let us name his new dog. I said Rudy and Easton suggested Ratchet, so Papa named him Rudy Ratchet. Rudy sits, counts, chases his tail, plays dead, rolls over, herds cows, protects the barn cats, keeps the ducks and chickens safe, and is

an all-around good dog. When Papa passed away, Rudy came to live on my uncle's farm. He seems happy. He reminds me of Papa Alfred.

Today Easton and I plan on working on the boat. Last night we made a list of all the things we need to take to Nana and Papa's house. Because it's so hot, we decided to take a tarp to use as a canopy. Uncle Melvin is not working today. He is a fireman and today is his day off. He said he would help us fix up the boat. Uncle Melvin is a kid in a man's body.

Mom is going to be proud of me when I tell her I've already written in my journal today. No timer today! I got up with the roosters to write. Too bad roosters can't write. Oh, I hear people getting up. Maybe the roosters woke them up too. I'm going to see if I can go scare Easton awake. He's usually up before me. Wish me luck!

Dear Summer,

Oh man, do I have a story for you! We just got to Nana and Papa's house. The adults are working on clearing out the house. No one lives there anymore so the water line was turned off. By the time we got to the house, I had to go to the bathroom BAD! I went inside to use the bathroom and Mom went out to turn on the water line. As I was in the bathroom going #2, the disconnect hose where the washer used to be started flying everywhere

and sprayed me with water from head to toe! Water went everywhere. The house was flooding and I was trying to go to the bathroom. I pulled myself together and ran out of the house yelling to my mom that the house was flooding. By this time, there was water in the hall, kitchen, bathroom and dining room. Mom finally heard me and turned the water off. She came back into the house and the water had made a huge mess. Later, Aunt Jamie, Uncle Melvin, and Easton showed up. We grabbed every blanket and towel available and started soaking up water. Uncle Melvin told my mom that she sure had a weird way of mopping the floor. I was so scared. I thought that by flushing the toilet, I had unleashed the water. Cleaning up was fun. Easton and I used the tile in the house as an indoor water slide.

Dear Summer,

The man boat has officially been created! Uncle Melvin didn't help Mom and Aunt Jamie work in the house. He likes to play and decided that building the boat would be more fun. He brought lots of power tools, and we went into Papa's shop and grabbed everything we could think of to work on our boat. Uncle Melvin helped us tear out everything in the boat except the steering wheel and seats. Then he found some extra carpet in Papa's shop. We put the carpet down and then used Nana's old rugs to

line the sides of the boat since the metal gets hot. Uncle Melvin installed a long board right in the middle of the boat, and we nailed an old tarp to the top of it and used it as a canopy. Then Uncle Melvin found some Christmas lights and we streamed the lights around the edge of the boat. This is really looking good! It seems Papa Alfred knew we were going to need all of this stuff for a man boat clubhouse someday, because he had it lying around. Papa Alfred's workshop is the ultimate shopping place when looking for things to build a creation like this! Uncle Melvin took us in the woods and showed us the tree house he built when he was our age. He said that a boat would be much better. Easton found an old fish locator in the shop and it still worked! It made all kinds of beeping noises, and Uncle Melvin said we could use it so we mounted it to the boat. We are going to use it as a secret hand scanner. In order to enter the boat, you have to scan your hand to make sure that you aren't a zombie. We don't need zombies taking over our man boat!

Uncle Melvin mowed around the boat and removed the weeds. Snakes are really bad out in the pasture. Someone down the road got bit by a pygmy rattler. His hand swelled up as big as a softball. They put a picture of it in the newspaper. It made me stay on the lookout for creepy crawlers! Easton said he isn't afraid, but I sure don't want to get bit by that OR ANYTHING ELSE!

To top off our masterpiece, Uncle Melvin installed electricity! He found a really long extension cord and ran it from Papa Alfred's shop to the boat. We have ELECTRIC! Can you believe it? He also made us a zip line

that goes from a tree to the boat. It isn't ver

it's fun. After that, Uncle Melvin said the rest ˅

us. He said he better get to work or my mom

going to have his hide. He said that if he didn't wo˯ ˑᴛhen

we would probably find his head mounted in our man

boat. That might look pretty cool!

So while Uncle Melvin worked with Mom and Aunt

Jamie in the house, we made a list of rules for the man

boat. Here's what we came up with:

Man Boat Rules for ALL Who Dare to Enter:

Rule #1: No Farting (It's a small space)

Rule #2: No Telling of Secrets Shared Inside the Boat

Rule #3: Only Authorized People Are Allowed

Rule #4: No GIRLS (moms are okay if they bring food)

Rule #5: Dogs Are Allowed

Nanny always bought us art kits. She loved to draw

and wanted to make sure we had the chance to draw

when we were at her house. We went into the house and

found some of our old art kits and put them in the man

boat. Now we had the perfect set up! The rest of our day

was spent playing in the boat.

Now I need to get some sleep. Mom says we have

another long day on the farm tomorrow. I can't imagine

having more fun! Uncle Melvin has to work at the fire

station, so he won't be able to help. This writing thing

really isn't bad. I think I'm writing too much, but I want

to be able to share my stories with Mrs. Magle and the class when I get back from summer break. Oh no, did I just write something about summer ending? I better quit for now.

Dear Amazing Summer,

You have not let me down! Just when I think I've reached the highest point of my summer, you surprise me again. Before Uncle Melvin left for the fire station this morning, he woke both of us up and said we would have a camp out in the man boat later this week. Farm life is so fun! There's no way we'd be able to camp out in an old boat where I live. Maybe Mom will just leave me here for rest of the summer. It's extremely hot and there isn't a swimming pool, but we are free to roam and play. A boy could get used to this! I guess it's nice to be half city boy and half country boy. Mom says since Dad is 100% city boy and she is 100% country girl that makes me half of each. Wait 'til Jimmy and Matthew hear about this! Got to go, Aunt Jamie made us biscuits and sausage gravy for breakfast. I LOVE the country life! At home we eat cereal, but Aunt Jamie says country boys need country meals so they can play hard during the day!

Dear Sad Summer,

Kevin, the turkey, died today because she ate a fishing lure. Uncle Melvin found her behind the barn. I guess it was shiny and she couldn't resist! We are having a funeral for her after lunch. Uncle Melvin will dig a hole with the tractor. Easton and I are going to go gather some rocks for Kevin's grave marker. Kevin was a good turkey. She was more like a dog than a turkey. Her face turned bright blue when she got mad or scared. I have to go now. We need to plan Kevin's funeral service.

Dear Summer,

Kevin would have liked her service. Uncle Melvin dug a hole with the tractor. So that we would have more guests, we sprinkled feed around the grave. The chickens came to pay their respects. Everyone told a story about Kevin and Rudy did a few tricks. We each buried Kevin with something shiny. Easton put in a nickel, I added a shiny bubble gum wrapper, Uncle Melvin tossed in an old key, Aunt Jamie laid down a spoon, and Mom took off one of her shiny metal earrings. We closed with a prayer and Uncle Melvin let the chickens finish eating before he covered Kevin using the tractor. Later that evening we had a campfire and went to pick blackberries before it got dark. Kevin loved to go to the blackberry patch!

Dear Ridiculously Super Summer,

Uncle Melvin is off for several days, and tonight we get to camp in the man boat. I'm so excited. I can't wait until it gets dark! As usual, I got up early because of the roosters. I'm laying here in Easton's top bunk writing because it's all I have to do. If I walk around, I might wake everyone up. I sure miss Kevin tapping on the window. Maybe she was trying to send me a secret message. Maybe she was letting me know that there was something stuck in her throat?

The last time we camped out, my parents rented a cabin at a camping resort. I've never camped out on the farm. Papa always talked about it, but we never actually did it. I wonder if we will make it without getting eaten by zombies or even worse—Big Foot.

Dear Scary Summer,

Uncle Melvin and Easton have left me in the man boat alone. They walked back up to the farmhouse to get some water. I'm supposed to stay behind to keep an eye on the campfire. The boat looks pretty cool in the dark. I bet Nana would have never guessed we would use her

old Christmas lights to decorate a boat for camping in her back yard. I also bet Papa Alfred wouldn't have imagined we would've carpeted the old yellow boat in the pasture either.

They sure have been gone a while. I bet it's been five minutes already! I'm starting to hear noises, so to keep my mind off of things I think I'll just keep writing. I thought a farm was noisy in the morning, but I think I'd much rather put up with morning noises over nighttime noises any day! Morning noises are cheery and wake you up. Night noises echo and make you not want to close your eyes. I hear the howling of coyotes and the sounds of crickets. It's like they are singing a song. Maybe they are practicing and plan on putting on a show for Big Foot. My dad and I watch the Messing with Sasquatch beef jerky commercials and I'm pretty sure Big Foot looks a lot like Sasquatch. What if Big Foot is waiting for me to come out of the boat? What if he knows that Uncle Melvin and Easton have left me behind? Will he just pick me up and eat me as a snack? Hopefully I'm too skinny. Surely I would not be worth the fight. I'm a camo belt in karate, but I don't know if I'm prepared to take on Big Foot!

I MAY miss my mom. She would know what to say. Even though she isn't an alien, I think she would know the secret to keeping Big Foot away. She knows everything! Why didn't she come? How come my dad didn't come to the farm with us? He could have stayed behind with me. Uncle Melvin has left me behind so Big Foot will be full by the time they get back. They

didn't go get water! They are just waiting on Big Foot to make his move and then BAM, Big Foot gets full and satisfied, and they get to camp without worrying about being eaten. I never thought that Uncle Melvin would leave me as Big Foot bait. First Kevin bites the dust and now me. That's probably the reason he installed electricity, he wanted to get Big Foot's attention. I bet they're just sitting up at Nana's waiting on the sounds of digestion.

Dear Summer,

I may have gotten a little carried away last night. It turns out that Uncle Melvin and Easton did go after water, and I wasn't left for consumption. We made it a full night in the man boat. Uncle Melvin told stories about fighting fires, and we made up camp stories of our own. We had a really good time and our man boat was so much fun. Today is my last day, and we'll leave tomorrow. After we get back from working at Nana and Papa's house, we are going to pick more blackberries and Uncle Melvin promised us a chance to ride four wheelers in his pasture.

Dear Super Summer,

We just left Uncle Melvin and Aunt Jamie's farm. I was sad to go, but I miss my dad. Even though he calls me every night, I'm so ready to see him. As we pulled out of the long drive, Rudy Ratchet followed us and kept jumping on the door barking at me. I think he was telling me not to go. I'm so tired. I think I'll sleep on the way back to Owasso. Mom said she'd stop in town and buy me a pack of gum before we get on the highway. Goodbye farm!

Chapter Four

Camp

Dear Bummer Summer,

After the alien incident, my mom signed me up for a four day camp. She said that "being idle" isn't meant for me, and I needed to stay busy this summer. CAMP? Who wants to go to camp? It would be okay if I was going with friends or even people I knew. It's probably a mind control camp. Mom has signed me up to have my brain reprogrammed so I'll stay out of trouble!

Dear Summer,

The camp doesn't sound so bad now. It's a church camp and the brochure I read mentioned that we will get to slide down a big inflatable waterslide, compete in a paintball war and nerf gun war, and will have a snack shack open several times a day. This should be okay. I'm still not sure about being gone a whole week though. I bet we'll have a schedule for every minute of our time. Not sure about meeting new people. That makes me nervous!

Dear Bummer Summer,

In one hour I'll be taken to a bus for church camp. What kind of parents put their only child on a bus without knowing much about the camp? My parents do not deserve to be parents of the year!

Dear Embarrassing Summer,

Oh my goodness! My mom just boarded the bus with me! MY MOM IS GOING TO CAMP! HOW COULD SHE DO THIS? I knew something was going on when she seemed really happy about leaving the house. I also thought it was

mysterious that she went shopping for new shorts and shoes before I left for camp. Most moms shop after their kids leave for camp. How did I miss the signs?

When we got to the parking lot where the bus was located, Mom stopped the car and said, "Gum, I have a great surprise for you! I'm going to camp too!" I felt like the Titanic just before it sunk! I broke in half on the inside and slipped down in my seat. I think I even barfed a little in my mouth. People won't like my mom. She'll schedule everything. She'll lecture them. She'll tell embarrassing stories about me. Oh no, my reputation can't afford to have stories told about me. How am I supposed to make friends? I never get a chance to break the rules. I hope she doesn't try to be my roommate or even worse— BUNKMATE! My life is over! I won't be able to recover from this. Why can't I have a normal mom like everyone else? She has way too much time on her hands. I've been emotionally sideswiped! Ripped off. Left for dead. H-U-M-I-L-I-A-T-E-D!

Dear Disgusting and Emotionally Crippling Summer,

I chose to sit in the back seat on the bus. I've placed my backpack in the seat next to me so that no one sits by me. My mom started off sitting in the seat across the aisle, but once the bus got moving, she looked really sick

and started turning green. One of the counselors saw her and moved a kid from the front to the back so Mom could sit in the front seat and have the air conditioner on her face. Now I have some kid with green hair sitting across from me.

Gum = 1, Mom = 0

The war is on! I will win.

I wonder why Dad didn't warn me about Mom going to camp. Maybe she really thought I'd be happy about the news and was really trying to surprise me with her jumping on the bus at the last minute. I don't care though. It wasn't right for her to do this to me. I'm sick of surprises!

Oh no! Mom is dancing on the bus. This is terrible! This is horrible! I think I'm gonna die right here and now. The bus driver started playing music and my mom is dancing up and down the aisle like she owns the place! Now she is fist bumping and telling the other kids to call her MOM! Gotta go. I'm going to pull my backpack over my head and try to camouflage myself into the corner. This will be the worst week of my entire life, and I'm not sure how I'm supposed to bounce back from THIS!

Dear Punch Me in the Gut Summer,

The bus arrived, we've unpacked and all kids were told to sit in their bunks for some quiet time before we had our

first meeting. The adults (including my mom) are meeting in the mess hall. I chose to get my flashlight and write. I'm pretty sure I won't survive and Dad needs to know how devastating this week was on me. I'd think that the person I refer to as Mom would give Dad my journal should I go missing. It's the least she could do!

The bunks are cool. I scored a top bunk in the back of the boy's dorm. The bunks are like mini trampolines and are connected to the bed frames with springs. I have to remember to jump on it later when no one is looking.

I haven't met anyone yet. The guy with the green hair looks cool, but I haven't seen him since we got off of the bus. Maybe I'll find him. Making new friends is tough. Not sure why mom and Dad didn't arrange for a friend to come with me. This place would be a lot more fun if Matthew, Jimmy, Austin, or Easton came too.

Dear Summer Who Must Hate Me,

It's time for bed, but I must tell you what's happened! The camp host met with everyone and went over the rules and then they had all of the camp counselors stand up and go to the front for introductions. My mom is one of the camp counselors! She planned this and has obviously been planning this for quite some time. Each counselor was assigned a family of campers. Mom was assigned number two, the white group. They told us

that after chapel they would number us off on our way out and that would be our new "family group" for the entire week.

At first I thought I had this in the bag. There were twelve groups and there was NO WAY I was going to get teamed up with my mom. I sat in chapel by myself and they dismissed the counselors to go stand outside by their group shelters to wait for us as we were assigned to our families. I tried really hard to control the situation. I thought I had it taken care of. I paid really close attention to the camp hosts at the door, I counted off people at the door to make sure that I was any number BUT TWO. Just then, I was about to be selected as a number one and BAM! The dude with the green hair jumps in front of me, distracts me, and says "Hi, my name is Zane. What is your name?" Next thing I knew, I was a TWO. Battleship sunk! Part of me thought about switching with someone, but I didn't know anyone else and green haired guy a.k.a. Zane ran off to shelter number one to be with his new family.

So I walked, slowly I walked over to shelter two where my mom was standing cheering on every new camper that entered her group. Her face lit up like a Christmas tree when she saw me. As I got closer, she started jumping up and down clapping her hands. Then she started cheering "GUM, my precious gumdrop!" Everyone looked my way and seemed confused. One guy started laughing at my name. Then someone asked the question: Why do you call him Gum? My super hero mom told the entire group about how I got my nickname.

My dad likes gum and since I was really little I would beg for gum, hide gum in my room, and would even sneak gum to school. So the name stuck like a piece of gum. Everyone laughed. I thought they were laughing at me, but they were laughing at my mom. My mom was funny! I laughed and then lots of people came to sit by me. I suddenly had friends. I was the cool kid!

GUM = 1, Mom = 1

Once Mom got the other kids seated under our shelter, she came over and whispered in my ear. She said, "Gum, I can get you out of my group and put you in another group. I didn't plan to be your counselor at camp. I want you to relax here and have fun and not worry about me being right behind you every second." I had to think quickly. On one hand I didn't want Mom as my counselor, but on the other hand I'd made several friends. I was expected to be cool, and people knew my name. I just shook my head no. My mom smiled and she started teaching her class. I didn't participate, but my new friends did.

After our group meeting, Mom dismissed us and told us we had free time to swim, play tennis, or even just hang out. I didn't want for the group time to be over because I thought that my new friends would leave me, but they didn't. They stayed by my side. To top it off, they told me I had a very cool name and they wanted to have nicknames too. They asked ME to give them cool names like mine. What a cool gig? I got to create names. I told them I needed to know more about them so their new names reflected who they were. One of them said

they liked pop, so I named him Fizz. Another guy said he loved reading, so I called him Word. The last dude said he lost his pinky finger when he was little, so I named him Digit. Everyone liked their names so we decided to go swimming. The cool thing about being a boy is that you always have on swimming shorts. We can swim in anything. DUDES RULE!

I better get some sleep. We have to get up early. This is awesome and so exciting! I can't wait to tell Dad about my new friends.

Dear Summer,

Right now is bunk time. We each have to go to our bunks for personal devotion time. I practiced my memory verses and now have 20 minutes left, so I thought I'd write in my notebook to pass the time.

This morning I woke up and heard lots of noises in the bathroom. There were several teen sponsor guys in there trying to capture a snake that had made its way into our dorm. I was kind of scared, but I wanted to see too. Good thing my bunk is right across from the boy's bathroom. It doesn't smell great, but I got to see all of the action! They brought the snake out and it was just a little garden snake. When I get home I'll research the snake on the Internet and find out exactly what kind of snake it was.

I met my new friends in the mess hall and we ate breakfast together. Fizz, Word, and Digit all liked biscuits and gravy just like me. They told me I had a cool mom. Where did that come from? I guess she isn't so bad now. She really hasn't bothered me much, and she has to sleep in the girl's dorm because there are no girls allowed in the boy's dorm. That's a pretty cool rule. Speaking of rules, you can chew gum here! There's gum stuck to everything.

After breakfast there was an announcement that anyone wanting to play paintball had to go to the deck for a meeting. So the gang and I ran to the deck and waited. This cool camp guy named Zeek brought out a mask, gun, and some paintballs. He told us everything about paintball and what to expect. He even said that someone shot him at close range once in the neck and it caused him to pass out. Zeek is really tall. I bet that sounded like a tree falling in a forest. Geez! He said that if you shoot someone in the neck, then you can't play for rest of the week. We get to play later, and I'm excited. All of my friends agreed to be on the same team and not shoot each other. Devo time is over. I'm outta here!

Dear Summer of Surprises,

I think I actually like church camp. Today was freakin' awesome! We had three hours of on your own time. Fizz

got a pop at the canteen and while he was drinking it, Word was telling us something funny he read about in a magazine and Fizz blew Mountain Dew out of his nose! We all laughed so hard. He was a human sprinkler. He even sprayed some girls who were sitting near us and they took off screaming and went to tell their counselor that we were being gross. Fizz really is a good name for him.

After lunch today the camp host came over the speaker and yelled out "MAIL CALL"! Everyone started screaming and ran into the dorms. I followed them, and they all put on their swimsuits, so I put on mine too. Digit came to camp last year and said that if you got a package or three letters at camp, then you were thrown into the pool by two of the adults. Digit said he was thrown about 20 feet in the air last year. That sounded fun, but I didn't know who would send me a package at camp. My dad came through though. He made me a package and mailed it to camp. I was so excited. I got a package at camp! Inside the package was beef jerky, FIVE PACKS OF GUM, candy and a letter from my dad. I have to remember to tell Dad thanks when I get home. It was kind of sad because Word didn't get a package today. He tried to not let it bother him. I guess his parents didn't know about the packages. I told him there was always tomorrow. He cheered up. I hope he gets a package!

Getting thrown in the air by two really big dads was so awesome! Mom took a picture of me in mid-air, and I looked like I was a kung-Fu master! Dad is really gonna like that picture. I wish Easton was here with us. He

would like my new friends. Mom said he couldn't come because he was going to be in the middle of a baseball tournament.

We lined up for paintball, but the line was too long. Digit told us they would have it tomorrow, so we all went to the tennis court and made up our own game. The four of us even made up our own language that only we understood. Afterwards, I brought Fizz, Word, and Digit into the dorm and shared my gum with them. They thought it was pretty cool of my dad to send gum to camp. We spent a lot of time talking about dads, and I told them about the time my dad was chased by an emu and they all laughed.

Lights are going out in two minutes. I NEED sleep. We have to get sleep for paintball tomorrow. PAINtball! It does hurt! I'm kinda scared.

Dear Funtastic Summer,

It's Devo time in our bunks again. My new friends traded bunks with some other kids and now Word is directly under me and Fizz and Digit are sharing a bunk next to us. We are like one big family! Fizz lives in Kansas, Digit lives in Arkansas, Word lives in Missouri, and I live in Oklahoma. We are all from four different states. All of them got sent to camp alone by their parents also. I think Fizz is starting a journal about camp too. He said

he doesn't like to write, but when I told him why I was writing, he decided that he could try it.

I guess I am not so mad anymore about Mrs. Magle making us write in our writer's notebooks. It's been kind of good for me, and I think I like it (just a little).

Today is the day for paintball. I have to go now. Word is going to jump up on my bunk and bring his flashlight. We're gonna have a flashlight war on the ceiling until devo time is over.

Dear Summer,

Today was AwEsOmE! We entered paintball as a team and we didn't win, but we didn't get shot in the neck and pass out either. We chose to be the white team. The course was made in the middle of a forest. It was so cool! There were a bunch of girls who decided to play paintball in their swimsuits. I'm not sure what they were thinking, but we shot them and they all dropped their guns and ran out. I don't think they'll be coming back to the paintball course.

I think Word may read too much. He said he thinks he saw Big Foot lurching in the woods. The rest of us heard something, but we didn't see anything. I was hiding behind a tree and saw something move about 10 feet from me. I put my gun down to go check it out. It was a nest of about 20 baby bunnies. They weren't very old

because they still had their eyes closed. When the guys came to look for me, they got to see the bunnies. None of the other guys had ever seen baby bunnies like this before, but my Papa Alfred used to raise them so I knew that we shouldn't touch them. I was worried someone would step on them while playing paintball, so I sent for someone to go get Zeek, the giant camp counselor. Zeek said we couldn't move them, and we should leave them alone. Kind of wish I didn't say anything because Zeek shut down that part of the paintball course. He said it was more important the rabbits be left alone. I wonder how long it will take for those rabbits to leave their nest. I never really thought about rabbits having a nest. I only thought that birds had nests.

I got shot in the hand with a paintball gun and it made my hand bleed. It wasn't a lot of blood, but everyone thought that it was cool I got shot and it brought blood.

Word still didn't get a package during mail call today, so we decided to put a package together while he was taking a shower. We each added something special to the package. I'm not sure how we will get it in the mail, but I bet we can figure it out. We used the same box that my dad used for my package and just crossed off my name and wrote "Word" across the top. I'm sure he will figure out who sent it, but at least he will get tossed into the pool. He seemed bummed today. Maybe Mom can help us somehow.

As for me, I haven't showered since the day before we left for camp. I don't really see a need. The swimming pool is a big bathtub, and I'm sure the chemicals in the

pool will erase any dirt deposits I have on my body. There's this kid named Brody and he just doesn't like water. He hasn't bathed and hasn't gone swimming the entire time we've been here. He doesn't smell good, and he's in our family group. His mom is going to be mad when she picks him up from camp! My mom would make me walk home.

There are other things that don't smell great. Maybe getting the bunk next to the only boy's bathroom wasn't a smart idea. It smells so bad! I'm trying to breathe through my mouth, but I forget. It smells like a skunk. Not just your ordinary skunk either. I'm talking about one of those "mad at you forever and out to get you skunks". One of the counselors told us there were 140 boys sharing the same dorm and we needed to flush the toilets and clean up after ourselves. I started off not showering just because and now I'm not showering because the bathroom is grosser than being dirty. The girls won the cleanest dorm today. They announced that their bathroom wasn't full of flies. The girls have TWO bathrooms in their dorm, and they don't have to sleep on spring cots. They have mattresses. GIRLS ARE SO LUCKY!

Mom is looking tired. She isn't bothering me much. All of the girls seem to like her and last time I saw her, she was sitting in the middle of a group of girls braiding their hair. I'm not sure where she learned to do something so fancy. She surprises me sometimes! I just hope that the girls don't think she puts makeup on me and stuff at home. I'm very tired and must sleep. Lights go out in a few minutes. ZONK time!

Dear Summer,

Today is the last day of camp. It wasn't so bad, and my mom didn't bother me as much as I thought she would. I think she made a new friend too. She met some lady named Miss Melissa and they have the same birthday. Good for her! This is our last devotional time in our bunks and then we have to pack up our things and load up on the bus.

This will be the last time I see my new friends, but we swapped addresses and promised to keep in touch. I'm hoping our parents let us Skype or email. That would be cool. I really didn't think I'd have this much fun, but I did.

Dear Summer,

We are loaded on the bus, but one of the campers is missing. My mom went to find them. I'm sure they just got on the wrong bus. The teen girl counselors said we are going to dance on the way home. I think I'll draw. I'm not much into dancing.

Chapter Five

Rocket's Red Glare and Bombs Bursting in Air

Dear Sultry Summer,

It's so hot outside! Mom and I just did the "fry an egg outside" experiment and it worked. That means we need to stay inside during the hottest part of the day. My buddy Matthew came over and we played Minecraft for several hours and then built a huge fort in the guest bedroom. The heat must be getting to my mom because she said we could keep it up all summer long or at least as long as I kept writing. She doesn't know I've been

writing almost every day and sometimes two times per day. After the alien incident, she quit setting a timer at the table. Maybe I scared her.

Dear Summer,

The ultimate father son holiday has arrived—finally. Fourth of July is right around the corner. This is the only time of the year we get to blow up things. My dad is the best firework blaster ever! There's a plus to being the only older boy other than Matthew on the street. The girls on my street don't like to light fireworks. They just like to watch, so their dad's buy fireworks and I get to light them. I think I may explode into a million pieces from all of the excitement!

Fireworks are funny and mysterious. I'm not really sure how all those colors get packed into a paper cone or missile, but when they go off and explode in the air it's amazing. Someday I'd like to learn more about how they actually work. Mrs. Magle told us we get to choose research projects of our own about any topic, and I may pick this topic. It will be a tough decision though, because I also want to know how all of the water gets reused on Earth, the mystery behind the Bermuda Triangle, and why bats always exit a cave in the same direction. I wonder if I could combine these topics into one report. Some kids in my class don't like to write, but I'm thinking

that writing is like exploring except instead of physically doing this stuff; I get to let my imagination explore the cave of my brain.

Dear Summer That Keeps Getting Better,

Mom is going to Oklahoma City for a teacher conference. She needs to get better about sharing her calendar with me, because I didn't know this was happening either. How would she like it if I just mentioned I was leaving one day with no real warning? I was mad at first, but then it hit me like a rock! I realized this meant I was being left in the hands of my dad during the Fourth of July holiday. There will be NO MOM to supervise our events. I better go help her pack—quick!

Dear Super Spectacular Summer,

Mom is packed. Mission blast off is about to begin and then my dad will have his hands full. She's leaving tomorrow and will be back in four days. That's plenty of time to do what we need to do. Mom is always overprotective when it comes to fireworks. She acts like she is the master of safety. Who needs safety when I have my dad?

Dear Summer,

Mission blast off has started! We just put Mom's bags in her car, and we both kissed her good-bye. She suspects nothing! I sort of wonder what's going on in Dad's head. What does he have planned? He told me to stay here while he went to return some tools to the neighbor. I can only imagine. Maybe the neighborhood dads are really planning some huge Fourth of July party!

Dear Summer,

We get to go to the firework stand this afternoon. I asked Dad how many fireworks we could buy and he said that the sky was the limit. Oh boy! This is going to be the best Fourth of July EVER!

Dear Remarkable Summer,

My dad is the best! Today we went to not one, not two, but THREE firework stands. Dad shelled out over $500 on fireworks. We loaded up the back of the truck. Dad

let me put the fireworks in the garage since Mom's car wasn't home. We have day fireworks on one side and night fireworks on the other side. There was even a firework called "Dancing Gum Drops". Of course we had to get that one! We'll begin our four day firework vacation tonight. I can't wait! I have to go. We need to go eat because Dad doesn't cook. Erin's mom has invited us over for dinner. She does that a lot when my mom is gone. I think she feels sorry for us. I don't mind because I like spending time with Erin.

Dear Summer,

Last night was stinking awesome! All of the neighbors sat out on the lawn while we lit some night fireworks. Everyone enjoyed the show. Erin, Maddie, and Catie clapped every time we set off a firework. I guess they really liked them. Matthew had company, and he didn't get to come outside. The parachutes were really cool. We set off some night snakes that glow in the dark as they grow. As we watched them, we made up snake stories in the dark and that was fun. Maddie doesn't like snakes, so she started talking about princesses and unicorns. It was okay though. I didn't want her to be scared, so I helped her and our story ended up being about snakes turning into unicorns. Tomorrow will be the grand finale! Tomorrow is the Fourth of July, and we will pop all of

our fireworks then. Mom won't believe it when I tell her how many fireworks we popped and that we popped fireworks for FOUR STRAIGHT DAYS!

Dear Summer,

I am not sure where I should begin. Right now we are staying in a hotel. I will have to write later. Mom is coming back from her trip now, and she isn't happy! Dad just came back from the police station. Grandma Jo checked us into a hotel and stayed with me until Dad got back.

Dear Summer,

Apparently, there are certain fireworks that shouldn't be done in town. Dad was given a $1,000 fine for shooting off illegal fireworks within city limits. He also has to pay a fee to the city for putting out the fire. YES, I SAID FIRE! Mom is going to be really upset. I'll give details later. Not sure why Mom left us alone with fireworks. You would think she had more sense. She knows Dad loves this holiday and gets too carried away.

Dear Summer,

It looks like we'll be at the hotel for about a week. Mom is here and this is our second night in the hotel. The hotel doesn't have a swimming pool and Mom and Dad are talking with our insurance company over the phone. Mom isn't real happy about the situation. You would think she would be a little bit happy since we rescued her from a teacher conference. She isn't! I'm staying away from her because she has this strange look on her face. Dad tried to talk to her, and she said she wasn't ready to chit chat about our adventure just yet. It's very stressful around here. To make it worse, we are in a tiny hotel room and Mom is very wound up and angry. She isn't talking to us much, but she keeps talking to the dog. What she says to the dog is really meant for us.

Dear Doom and Gloom Summer,

Mom is doing better today. She hugged both of us and said she was glad no one got hurt. Dad pulled me aside and told me to act scared and frightened and she might go easy on us. Not sure how I like being used as a decoy, but I owe Dad. Even looking back it was still awesome! Mom wants to hear the whole story later when she gets back from meeting with the construction crew. Dad and I are going to meet to get

our story straight. Poor Dad! He never should've bought that many fireworks. Mom would've read the firework packaging.

Dear Smokey Summer,

Mom and Dad are gone and I've been taken to Grandma Jo's for a couple of days while they work out all the details to put our house back together again. I guess I need to document what really happened in case Mom decides to put an end to us for good. She isn't as mad now and seems to be cool and thankful we are alive. She said we put a lot of people in danger with our "antics". I'm not sure what an "antic" is, I'll check the word later.

We were having a blast! We'd just eaten at Maddie's house and watched the city firework display. All of the neighbors came over, and we were about to put on our grand finale display. I had just taken out several fireworks from the garage to light in the street. Dad was lining up the night works, and he asked me to shut the garage door. As the garage door was shutting, Dad fired up a big firework he thought was a small fountain named "Rocket's Red Glare". Apparently it wasn't a small fountain! It was a 50 shell missile launcher. As Dad turned to walk away from the firework, he knocked it over on its side with his shoe. He didn't realize his

mistake until it was too late. At the same time the missile started going off, the garage door was shutting. The missile timed its entrance into the garage just right. About 15 launches went straight into the garage and shot up into the hot water heater and exploded. The other 35 or so launches pounded into the metal garage door and sounded like a machine gun being fired directly at our house.

Dad didn't open the garage door right away. He and the other parents cleared the yard and moved everyone over to Matt's house across the street. Then I saw my dad walk over to the house to open the garage door. Before he opened it, we heard the sound of what seemed to be a firework orchestra playing some REALLY loud music. We heard zings, bangs, poofs, and thuds. Everyone stood across the street with their mouths open, and Maddie's dad panicked and called 911. They dispatched a fire truck. The area of the house near the garage started going up in flames. Smoke was rolling out of the garage when the firemen opened the garage door. Fireworks were zipping through the garage. Dad's mower caught on fire too and exploded.

At least it didn't catch the entire house on fire. The firemen did a really good job putting out the fire. Not only did we get "Rocket's Red Glare", but I am pretty sure we got the bombs bursting in air also. Mom doesn't see the humor in it yet.

Dear Big Bang Summer,

I'm getting really tired of the hotel room. I can't wait to get back home. Apparently the fire was kept to the garage and MY BEDROOM. My room shares a wall with the garage. Both rooms were torched! The upstairs got a little bit of smoke damage in the area directly above my room, but Mom said it wasn't bad up there. I didn't get to look at the upstairs because it was unsafe. Mom and Dad took me over to look at the house. The fire torched all of my clothes in my closet also, but none of my Legos melted, so I am cool. Mom said I grow like a weed anyway and needed new clothes. Now I have to go clothes shopping. BARF! Mom is excited about that part. She told Dad she was going to shop also and treat herself. Dad didn't disagree.

Dear Blazing Summer,

Come on with the heat! Enough already! The ground is so dry that it's cracking! I miss my house. We get to go back home in two more days. Apparently the company Mom hired has been working like crazy to get the house finished so we can at least get back inside. Maybe they are afraid of my mom too!

Hotels don't like dogs much. We had to take Lizzy to stay with my Grandma Jo. I miss her a lot. When I sleep,

she curls up in bed with me. She isn't a "sleep at the end of the bed" kind of dog either. She sleeps at the head of the bed on her own pillow and has to be covered up and tucked in each night. If you don't tuck her in, she barks and barks loud until she is treated like a human. I hope that Grandma Jo tucks her in right or she won't get any sleep.

Dear Summer,

We're home! I really don't want to stay in another hotel ever again, and I think that I'd much rather watch fireworks from my chair next year. Mom said from now on we are limited to smoke bombs, snakes, snappers, and tanks unless she approves them and the garage door is SHUT!

Dad went back to work and things are sort of back to normal. Mom has begged me to keep things on the "down low" for a while. I guess I owe her that much! So now I have to be a boring kid. We're only half way through summer. I don't know how long I'll be able to keep up with BEING A FAKE.

ChapteR Six

Three-Dimensional Horror Graphics

Dear Boring Summer,

I've been so good for about a week. I've helped my mom and have stayed out of her way. Of course she has told everyone about what happened to our house. The house is almost finished, and I'm close to moving out of the guest bedroom and back into my room. All they have to do is paint. Setting your room on fire is kind of cool, because you get a brand new one. I picked out my bedroom color and chose blue. I think blue is a good color.

Mom says it may keep me calm, but I'm not sure if that'll happen. Dad says it isn't possible.

My parents just told me that we are going to Mexico for vacation. Mom said she needed to be on a beach somewhere. That'll be fun, but I'm not sure about going to a place where another language is spoken. How am I supposed to eat? I've been assured that English will be spoken in most of the places we'll go. Both Mom and Dad used to take vacations there, but this will be my first visit. I had to go get my picture taken for my passport. They don't let you smile for your passport photo. It took about 25 tries to get "an approved" photo. Mom kept yelling "Gum, quit smiling in your picture!" That just isn't a natural thing to say to a child. I get in trouble when I don't smile in my school pictures and BAM; I get in trouble for smiling for a vacation photo. There needs to be more balance in this world, and I'm sure some adult made up that rule!

Dear Relaxing Summer,

It has been brought to my attention that we're going to see The Lion King live performance at the Performing Arts Center. First of all, that sounds stupid. The last live performance I saw was Elmo, and I was four years old. I think my parents enjoyed it more than I did. Second, Dad is just doing this to smooth Mom over so she'll quit

talking about fireworks every time he fires up the BBQ grill. I'm not sure why I have to be caught up in the middle of their drama. Things are going fine for me. We don't need to go see people dressed as animals dancing on a stage for three hours.

Dear Interesting Summer,

I have an idea, and it is a good one if I do say so! Matthew and I are going to create a solution that will make me invisible and then when we go see the performance I'll simply transform into my invisible self and go on stage. No one will ever know that I was part of the production. This should be interesting!

Dear Invisible Summer,

Today I had my mom take me to the library. She was thrilled that I wanted to read, so it was not a problem at all. She spent the entire time in the giggle section of the library. You know the area where all the moms go to read and they smile like someone is telling them jokes. Yeah, that section!

I found two books with formulas for disappearing

solution. I can't wait to try them out to see if they work! Matthew is going to help. We might even be able to use the solution at school. I could probably even sell it on the playground.

Dear Scientific Summer,

Matthew spent the night last night, and we worked on the invisible solution. It was made of lemon juice, Windex, and vinegar. We put it in my water gun and drenched each other. It didn't work. We were both kind of bummed, and I only have two more days to find out how to make myself invisible. Matthew is going to work on a solution at home also. Tonight I am going to try the other solution.

Dear Not-So Scientific Summer,

Well, the invisible solution never worked. I couldn't find a solution that even made me disappear for just a little bit. Oh well, I guess I'll go and sit through the entire performance. They should punish adults for making kids endure events like this.

Dear Embarrassing Summer,

I was set on going to the performance and doing my best by being "obedient". It just didn't work out that way. I'm not sure this is really my fault though. Things started off good. Dad and I dressed up and Dad told me from the start that this night was for Mom. He said she needed this after the firework incident. I agreed. I could see he was walking on a thin sheet of ice. He had a look of desperation in his eyes, and I felt he just needed me to go along for man support.

The show opened up and to my surprise it was awesome! People in amazing costumes were coming down the aisle dancing and a huge elephant was gliding through the air above our seats. Mom's face glowed with happiness! For a moment, I thought things wouldn't be so bad after all. Boy was I wrong!

During the first intermission, Dad bought me a soda. It was big! I could barely hold it in my lap. I was frozen in amazement during the second act. I guess I just locked my lips on my straw and sucked the entire drink down. I sat my empty cup on the floor under my seat and a few moments later, I found myself needing to go #1 really bad. I had to pee so bad I started wiggling in the seat. I leaned over to Dad and told him I had to go and he asked me if I remembered seeing the bathroom on the way in. I could tell he didn't want to leave. He was holding Mom's hand, and she was smiling. I'm not even sure he remembered I was with them until I told him I needed to go to the bathroom. He nodded at me as if

to say "go on". So I got out of my seat and headed for the john.

As I left the auditorium and went into the lobby, I spotted the restroom. No problem. This seemed easy. I get in and out, then back to my seat. NOPE! Not so simple. As I was coming out of the restroom, I saw Jimmy. He was in the lobby. His mom works at the event center and sometimes she lets him come to work with her. He gets to sit in the back of the auditorium and watch as long as there is an empty seat. Apparently he saw me and was waiting for me just outside the restroom.

We got to talking, and he asked me if I wanted to see something cool. OF COURSE I SAID YES! I love a good adventure! I figured my mom and dad would hardly notice my absence. I would be quick like lightning! Jimmy knew everything about the event center. He knew all the secret doors. It was almost like we were walking in between the walls. I could hear the performance beating through the walls. BOOM! BOOM! BOOM! Jimmy introduced me to some of the event staff, but they were really busy so we kept moving. I just followed Jimmy. At one point, I could see the performance down below. Somehow we made it all the way above the audience and were walking on a metal walkway which was attached to the ceiling by chains. It was swaying back and forth, back and forth. Jimmy was using his body to move the walkway. At first it was fun, and then I started feeling a little woozy. Woozy may not even be the right word for what I was feeling. I told Jimmy to stop, and he said that we weren't going to

get caught and then it happened. Three-dimensional horror graphics became part of the show. I puked all over the audience! We had just eaten Mexican food prior to the show, and I also sucked down about a gallon of pop. It was everywhere—fajitas, chips, queso, and LOTS of liquid! People started screaming and yelling. Then they began to get up out of their seats. The performance gradually came to a stop. I kept puking! It wouldn't stop! I turned around thinking I could stop, but instead I just puked on the other side. I was feeling sick, very sick. Jimmy grabbed me and pulled me to the side and there were several people waiting on us. One of the guys knew Jimmy's mom and took us to her immediately. Jimmy's mom was so mad! The show came to a complete halt. I didn't even want to see my parents. I knew I would be slaughtered or even worse, sold to an overseas sweat shop where kids do nothing but make sneakers. This would've been the perfect time for that invisible solution!

Jimmy's mom called my mom on her cell phone and said to meet her in the lobby. There they were, in the lobby, looking very angry. Mom was crying, and Dad was mad. No one was concerned as to why I puked. Jimmy had to come home with us because his mom had to deal with her boss. He said she would probably lose her job and that we had really done it this time. My parents didn't talk to me. They were really quiet on the way home. I felt so bad. Jimmy and I both just stared out of the back seat windows. I still felt sick to my stomach and even started to puke once, but swallowed it instead.

I didn't want to take a chance on making another mess. As soon as we got home, Dad sent us each to a room. I was sent to my room, and Jimmy was sent to the guest bedroom.

After Dad got Mom settled and calmed down, he visited with both of us. Jimmy fessed up and said he saw me leave the auditorium and was just excited I was there. Jimmy is a good friend because he took the heat for the entire night. I owe him big! Dad was afraid of what Mom would do to me, so he explained clearly what it was that I needed to do. I was told to take a shower and go to bed. I'm not sure what's going to happen to Jimmy. I just heard Dad tell him that his mom would be here soon. I'm going to try and go to sleep before she gets here.

Dear Summer,

I can still taste the Mexican food in my mouth. I probably should have brushed my teeth last night before bed. Jimmy wasn't here when I woke up. I went downstairs and Mom was sitting at the table talking to Dad. I didn't want to interrupt, so I just came back to my room. I called Jimmy, and he said his mom got fired from the event center. I feel so bad. Maybe I should've puked in my shirt or something, but when you need to puke, you need to puke.

Dear Uncertain Summer,

Dad has informed me that I'll be working to make things right with Jimmy's mom. Dad is going to offer her a job at his office, but he said I needed to prove to her that I was sorry. I also went over to apologize to her. She accepted my apology and told me she'd never seen something like that happen before. She asked if I was okay and apologized for Jimmy encouraging me to go on our "adventure". She visited with my dad and she was thankful for the job. Apparently this all worked out because she wasn't home most of the time, and Jimmy spent a lot of nights by himself. Working for my dad will give her more time at home with Jimmy. I sure was glad Dad offered her a job.

While I was there, I asked to see Jimmy since our parents were visiting about the new job. Jimmy was up in his room, and he didn't look too happy. I told him I was really sorry and I never would have imagined I was going to puke all over the audience. Jimmy said it was ok. He said he was so excited to see me that he just freaked and wanted me to see the cool places he gets to go when he goes to work with his mom. He also said he was moving the metal walkway back and forth and was trying to scare me. He just didn't realize I'd provide three-dimensional horror graphics for everyone enjoying the stage show. Jimmy declared us "cool" and

he appreciated what my dad did for his mom. Jimmy said things will be a lot better at home since his mom will have a "normal" job. He said she complained about her job after every event. In a way, he thanked me for puking on his mom's job.

Chapter Seven

Jimmy's Birthday Bash

Dear Summer,

Since I've started working, I've managed to stay out of trouble. Of course I've had minor blips, but I'm only human. Jimmy's mom knows I'm sorry for getting her fired from her job. He sure seems happier. Today he worked with me. Dad had us mow the lawn. At first we made designs in the grass. We thought since we lived near the airport we could send messages to the pilots flying overhead, but we found out our yards aren't big enough. Plus, Dad didn't think it was too funny.

Dear Summer,

Jimmy's mom said we could have a birthday bash for his 11th birthday. She said money was limited, and we could have a party as long as we raise the money. So now we are party planners. This could be interesting! Jimmy's mom told us we could have a sleepover and invite five of our friends. We are going to be busy. Jimmy knows I'm an entrepreneur and so he asked me to help him think of ways to raise money. We have two weeks. I've got to get busy.

Dear Summer of Work,

We came up with a list of things we could do to raise money for Jimmy's birthday bash. I tried to run them by Dad, but he was busy at the time and said "sounds good". I've learned that if you really want to do something, you ask when your parents are busy. Approval stamp secured. Mission completed.

Ways To Raise Money for Jimmy's Birthday Bash:

1. Charge advanced admission to the party
2. Sell lemonade

3. Catch fish and sell them

4. Clean cars

5. Sweep porches

6. Pick up doggie poo

7. Mow lawns

8. Wash dogs

9. Clean windows

10. Remove weeds from flowerbeds for old people

That should do it! I don't see any reason why we couldn't raise $100 to have an awesome birthday bash for Jimmy's birthday. We really want to have enough money to invite Dan's Animal Kingdom. I read about it on the Internet, but it's expensive. That would be cool, but we need about $400 for a private party. Having Dan's Animal Kingdom come to Jimmy's house would be the BEST BIRTHDAY BASH EVER! Let the work begin!

Dear Animal Kingdom Summer,

We made the invitation list:

1. Matthew

2. Austin

3. Zach

4. Trey

5. Brayden

After lunch we are gonna get on the computer and make invitations. I'm not sure how you collect admission money for a birthday party, but hopefully it'll work out.

Dear Summer,

It's surprisingly easy to collect advanced ticket money to a birthday party. However, there is one slight problem. Jimmy got so excited about the animal kingdom visit that he told everyone Dan's Animal Kingdom would for sure be there. Now kids are just bringing money to us to help pay for the show. Even kids who never were invited are bringing money. Jimmy's mom said we could have five friends sleep over. She is going to flip when she hears we already have 11 kids coming to the party. Maybe they don't have to all spend the night. Maybe they can just come for the show. We didn't mention anything to Jimmy's mom about Dan's Animal Kingdom coming to her house. That may destroy our plans! So far we have $110. Word sure spreads in a small neighborhood. Catie and Maddie heard about animals possibly being at Jimmy's party and they are telling everyone. I guess it makes my job as birthday coordinator a little easier. They are riding around catching people playing in their yards. Kids are

giving them money on the spot. As far as I'm concerned, Catie and Maddie are hired. They're doing a good job.

Dear Summer,

In the last 24 hours, we have collected $320. We really don't have a list of everyone who is coming to the party though. Catie and Maddie just came to my house on their bicycles and emptied out their plastic purses on my front porch, and we counted the money. Mom came out and asked us what we were doing with that much money, and Catie blurted out we were raising money for the zoo. I didn't interrupt because my mom just smiled and walked away. Later in the day, Mom said it was nice we were collecting money to help the zoo. She seemed so happy that I didn't want to make her sad. In a way, we are collecting money for a zoo, but I'm pretty sure it isn't what she thinks. That mom of mine has a far-fetched imagination. One of these days I'm sure it will get her into some sort of trouble.

I did tell Catie and Maddie they did a great job and to stop collecting money. I told them we needed to raise the rest by selling lemonade. We decided the party will be next Saturday at 2pm. We still needed to raise $80 to have enough money for Dan's Animal Kingdom. I'm certain we'll get it and this covert operation is about to get real. Maddie and Catie seem to think we are going to

have fluffy animals. They didn't ask, so I'm not offering up extra information. I wondered why girls wanted to see reptiles. I didn't think anything about it until Maddie asked if there would be kittens and bunnies. Oops! I told her I didn't think so.

Dear Covert Operation Summer,

I'm so certain we'll raise the last $80 that I just called Dan's Animal Kingdom and booked our live show. The person on the phone sounded really young and just told us we needed cash at the time of the event and said they could be there at 2pm on Saturday. I didn't have Jimmy's address, so I just gave the boy on the phone my address. That was way too easy! This entire thing has been way too easy.

P.S. Today we are going to sell lemonade in my driveway. Catie and Maddie are going to help. Jimmy was taken hostage and was forced to go visit his grandma.

Dear Summer,

If you would've told me I would be working with two girls on bicycles with plastic purses to raise money for

Jimmy's Animal Kingdom Birthday Bash, I would have said you were lying. Never in a million years would I have believed you! Catie and Maddie have made this very easy. Catie's mom loves to help with lemonade stands and Catie's grandma bought her an actual lemonade stand last year. I don't know what it is about two girls that can get moms so excited, but I let it work for me. My mom thought it was so cute I wanted to help the girls with their lemonade stand that she made four gallons of lemonade and brought out some cups too. Erin's parents pulled up in their driveway and Erin ran out to see us. I guess she just got back from cheering because she was in her cheerleading getup and had her pom poms. Erin said she would help us and asked if this was for the zoo. We said yes, so Erin stood out by the street and cheered for cars as they drove by and almost all of them stopped. Now if Jimmy and I stood out by the street, people would drive slowly and watch to make sure that we didn't do something to their cars. I've learned a very important lesson today. I learned that if you need business for your lemonade stand, girls know what to do. Erin cheered, Catie collected the money, and Maddie poured the drinks. I just stood there with a sign. In four hours we raised $42, and I consider it a very good day at the lemonade stand. Mom kept coming out to take pictures. I think I scored some points with her too.

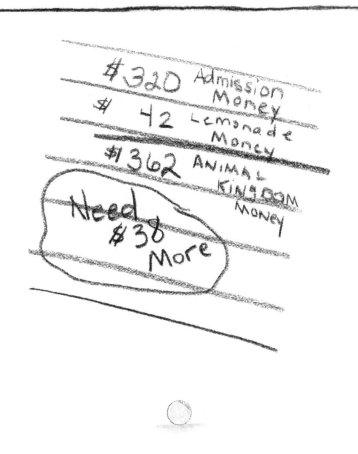

$320 Admission Money

$42 Lemonade Money

$1362 ANIMAL KINGDOM Money

Need $38 More

Dear Ultimate Party Summer,

Everything is going as planned. We still need the $38 so we can pay for the animal kingdom visit. I'm pretty sure it's okay to have the animals at the party. Jimmy's mom said we could plan a party with the money we raise, and my mom hasn't asked questions about the party. She just said it was nice we were raising money for the zoo. I'm going to assume that by zoo she means Dan's Animal Kingdom. She's been very tied up with her giggle book from the library. I don't know what she's reading, but

she laughs out loud every once in a while. Dad has been working a lot, and I've been left alone. Jimmy is still off visiting his grandma.

Erin said she would help me raise the last $38 and she would try and see if Rachel could come over to help also. Matthew has been on vacation and will be back tomorrow. Boy, Jimmy is going to be super excited! I better go. I told Erin I would meet her at the neighborhood park.

Dear Summer,

Today Erin, Rachel, and I made appointments to wash dogs. We are going to charge $5 per dog. We went door to door and told people about our services. We had two people who needed their dogs bathed. Mr. Yargold has two dogs, so that will give us $10. Mrs. Yancy across the street has a little yorkie that needs a bath. Mom said she would also pay us to bathe Lizzy. That should give us $20 total. We'll wash them tomorrow. Mom is taking me to swim, so I've got to go get ready. I can't wait until Matthew and Jimmy get back. They're gonna be shocked!

Dear Dog Washing Summer,

Rachel couldn't join us, so Erin and I started our day at Mr. Yargold's house. We brought a bucket, Lizzy's soap, mom's perfumed powder, and Dad's beach towel. Mr. Yargold's dogs are both tiny poodles. One's name is Tater and the other one is named Tot. Erin and I couldn't quit laughing! We were very nice, and Mr. Yargold seemed happy. He even told us if we wanted to come back next week that we could. I asked him if he needed his lawn mowed, and he said no. I think he drove by when we were mowing messages in Jimmy's yard for the pilots.

Next, we went to Mrs. Yancy's house. She has a Yorkie named Molly. Molly wasn't ready when we got there. Mrs. Yancy said Molly was watching television and she would be out when her show ended. Apparently Molly likes to watch Animal Planet. I didn't believe it, so I peeked in through the window and sure enough, there was Molly sitting on the couch with her eyes glued to the T.V. That was strange! Erin and I just waited on the porch. It felt strange waiting on a dog to finish a television show. When Molly was finished watching her show, Mrs. Yancy brought her out. Mrs. Yancy talked to Molly the entire time. She even told her she would take her to McDonalds to get a cheeseburger after she was finished. Molly seemed to know exactly what Mrs. Yancy was saying. She was a really good dog.

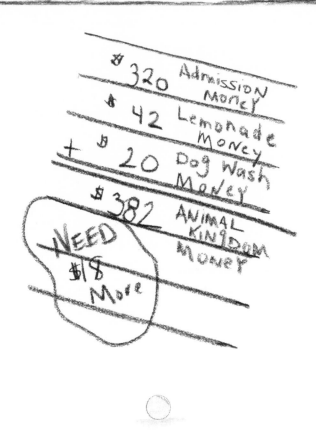

$$\$\ 320 \quad \text{Admission Money}$$

$$\$\ 42 \quad \text{Lemonade Money}$$

$$+ \$\ 20 \quad \text{Dog Wash Money}$$

$$\$\ 382 \quad \text{ANIMAL KINGDOM Money}$$

NEED $18 More

Dear Summer,

I can't raise money today because Mom asked me to go to the movies with her. She called it a date. YUCK! I think this means we are also going clothes shopping. I'm fine with the fact that Dad burned up my wardrobe and I only have a few things to wear. I can only wear one shirt and one pair of shorts at a time. Who needs lots of clothes?

Dear Summer,

Spending the day with my mom wasn't so bad. We went to see a 3-D documentary on extinction. It was pretty cool. She took me to Pizza Jack's for lunch and then we went to the mall. She said if I tried on clothes and cooperated that I'd get to make a trip to the candy store inside the mall. That only meant GUM, lots of GUM! So I agreed to the deal.

Now I just need to figure out how to make $18 for Jimmy's birthday party. The party is in two days! The pressure is building.

Dear Totally Awesome Summer,

Jimmy and Matthew are home, and we earned the $18 we needed! Jimmy can't believe it, and Matthew is so excited. Matthew has been gone on vacation the entire time, so all of this was a surprise for him. Mom woke up talking about work she needed to do around the house. I called Jimmy and Matthew and asked them if they wanted to earn some money. They said yes and so I told my mom we were trying to earn $18 for Jimmy's party. She laughed and said if we cleaned the windows, vacuumed, picked up after Lizzy in the backyard, and mowed the lawn that we could have our $18. So I mowed, Jimmy cleaned the windows and vacuumed, and Matthew didn't speak up fast enough so he got stuck with picking

up dog poo in the back yard. As a joke, we teased him and called him "Poo Poo Matthew"!

Mom paid us $20 which put us over the top, and we met our goal. I don't think she expected us to be so excited about $20. Jimmy's party is tomorrow! He said his mom was baking a cake for the party and that later they were going to get pop. All is a go!

Dear Birthday Bash Summer,

I just woke up. Today is going to be the coolest day ever! Dan's Animal Kingdom will be here in a few hours. I can hardly wait. Jimmy's mom asked us last night what we had planned for the birthday party because she knew my mom gave us $20. She also knew we had some money from the lemonade stand. Jimmy smiled at her and told her it was a surprise. She laughed and brushed us off. Boy, will she be proud!

Dear Ultimate-Fantastic-Super-Ridiculous-Amazing Summer,

We are all ROCK STARS! Everything went perfect for once in my life. As coordinator of the most amazing

birthday block party, I pat myself on the back. It was a little rough at first, but we managed.

Because I didn't know Jimmy's address, I had Dan's Animal Kingdom come to my house. Everyone was getting ready for Jimmy's party. His mom was setting out the cake and pop in the backyard and kids kept coming from all over the neighborhood. Maddie and Catie collected money from a lot of people. Apparently they made deals with kids that didn't have the full $10 and told them any donation would get them in the "zoo". Jimmy's mom froze at first and after the yard began to fill up; she just laughed and threw her arms in the air. My mom saw how many people were there and went to the grocery store and bought three more birthday cakes. I guess if you overwhelm parents enough, they just start to help and don't think twice about beating you over the head. My dad saw Dan's Animal Kingdom pull into our driveway and began to tell him he had the wrong house. I ran over to the house and explained the entire situation. Dan's Animal Kingdom was huge. He had three volunteers and lots of reptiles. I sort of had Dad on the hook. He didn't want to do anything to upset my mom, and he knew Jimmy's mom had been under enough stress so Dad was good to go. He patted me on the back and jumped into action. Dad helped Mr. Dan get everything unloaded at Jimmy's house. I paid Mr. Dan $400 and gave him a $2 tip. I figured he would be excited about the tip, but he wasn't. Also, there apparently was a limit on the number of kids. The party was supposed to be limited to 15 kids, and we quit counting at 42 kids. Erin tried her best to

keep track of the number of kids, but it was impossible. Adults came too. Everyone was curious. Even Mrs. Magle heard about the "zoo" and came over. She noticed my mom was gone and went right into teacher mode. She got everyone's attention and even had them sit in rows in the back yard.

Dan's Animal Kingdom was impressive! Mr. Dan told us all about the animals he brought and even let us hold them. I'm glad he had three volunteers. The coolest part was when he brought out a two headed boa constrictor named "Juice".

The party was a hit! My mom came to the rescue and bought enough cake and everyone had a good time. Jimmy's mom was relieved that my parents and Mrs. Magle showed up to help. All the parents were blown away at how well the party went. I guess you can do anything if you set your mind to it. Jimmy is officially eleven! Afterwards our parents did mention that next time they would like a warning, but they all laughed and said it was a pretty cool party. My parents were glad we did something good for Jimmy and his mom since my puke did cause her to get fired.

All in all, this was a pretty good day. We were so busy organizing the party we forgot all about the sleepover. I'm kind of glad. I think I've had enough adventure for a while. I'm going to call it quits as a birthday party coordinator.

Chapter Eight

Apples and Trees

Dear Summer,

I overheard Mom and Dad talking tonight, and it sounded like another adventure is soon to be on its way! Boy, you would think they wouldn't go anywhere with as many problems as they've had lately. I don't know how Mom does it. Dad causes all kinds of problems, and she still lets him go places. When I told her that, she said "the apple doesn't fall far from the tree". I'm not sure what that means. Mom doesn't buy very many apples.

Dear Summer,

My dad is the best! We get to go on an adventure with Uncle Melvin and my cousin Easton. He didn't tell me anything else. He said he still needed to work out some details with Uncle Melvin and is going to ask his work for a week of vacation. That's about the best news I've heard since Mom informed me she ordered dill pickle flavored bubble gum. It's supposed to be in any day, and I'm about to jump out of my skin. Dill pickles AND bubble gum? I may just explode!

Dear Summer,

It's a go! Dad is going to take a week of vacation and is taking me on an adventure with Uncle Melvin and my cousin Easton. Mom and Aunt Jamie aren't going. It will be a boy only adventure. Mom said I could go as long as I continue to write in my writer's notebook. She said she wanted to know all about the trip. I agreed. I like writing in my notebook anyway.

My Uncle Melvin is an outdoor guy. He loves to hunt, fish, farm, and about anything else done outside. My dad is more of a city guy. Mom calls him her "city slicker". Dad enjoys basketball, swimming in the pool, fireworks, movies, and wrestling with me. I can't remember ever going on an "all dads" trip before without the moms. This will be fun!

Dear Summer,

Uncle Melvin is friends with a man and woman who are camp hosts at Lake Tenkiller in Tahlequah. They had something come up and need to leave for a week. They didn't know who else to call, so they called Melvin. The couple asked if Uncle Melvin minded watching after the campgrounds while they were gone. They said we could stay in the main cabin at the lake. Of course Uncle Melvin jumped at the chance, and I'm glad he did. Dad told Uncle Melvin he could help too. Mom thought it would be okay and couldn't imagine we would find trouble at the lake in the middle of nowhere. I think she's right.

Dear Summer of Camping,

Today we packed for the lake. Dad sure packed a lot of stuff! I can't believe the things he packed. He packed DVD's, a BBQ grill, several newspapers, fishing poles, dog snacks, sleeping bags, and flashlights. The truck is loaded down! Mom just laughed.

I packed my clothes, the tackle box Papa gave me, swimming goggles and a snorkel, gum, my hat, sunglasses, and some beef jerky. Mom usually packs everything for

us, but she said she was busy and we were on our own. We are taking Lizzy because Easton is bringing his dog Jet. Lizzy and Jet are friends.

We leave tomorrow and I'm excited! Dad said I should get some good sleep. He said we'll have lots of work to do once we get to the campgrounds. I'm ready!

Dear Summer,

WE ARE HERE!

Dear SUMMER JOB,

Who would have thought being a camp host was so much work? As soon as we got here Uncle Melvin and Easton were already working. They laughed at all of the stuff we brought. Easton and Melvin each packed a bag and some fishing poles. Uncle Melvin said we looked like we were moving in and staying for good.

The camp hosts left us a list of what to do each day. The list is REALLY LONG! After we unpacked, we got in the golf cart and introduced ourselves to all of the people already camping. We also told them about the outdoor movie that would be playing at the amphitheater tonight

and invited them to come early so they could hear about the week's events. There will be a firework display on Friday. Uncle Melvin told Dad that some local people will come to light them. Dad and I both were relieved.

Tonight we met a funny old couple named Dee Dee and Roger. They travel all year long in their motor home and told us lots of stories about camping. Dee Dee invited us over for ice cream tomorrow. She likes to make homemade ice cream and asked us if we liked strawberry. Who doesn't like strawberry ice cream? Crazy people, that's who!

The movie was good. I had seen it before, but it was fun sitting outside. We didn't have a real movie screen. The camp hosts made one by painting the side of the restrooms white. We just had to hook up a laptop and portable projector. Everyone is nice here. Dee Dee and Roger sure laugh a lot during movies! She brought us popcorn.

Dear Summer,

When we woke up, there was a note on our cabin door telling us to go to Dee Dee and Roger's for breakfast. Dee Dee made biscuits and gravy. I think they feel sorry for us since we don't have our moms here. Roger mentioned something about fireworks, and I told them about Dad blowing up our house. They all laughed and

Roger said it was the best story he had heard in a long time. I think Dad was a little embarrassed I told it, but he was laughing too.

Uncle Melvin showed us how to split firewood. The camp provides firewood to all of its campers if they want it. When Uncle Melvin split a piece of wood, Easton and I collected it and tied it in bundles with rope. While we split and bundled wood, Dad worked the gate and checked in new guests. He checked in five new guests today!

Dee Dee makes the best ice cream. I don't know if it was because I was so hot and hungry or if she really did make the best homemade ice cream, but it tasted great! We didn't want to ask, but we all wanted seconds. I think she saw the look on our faces because she put more in our bowls when we finished the first helping.

While Dad and Melvin did more work, Dee Dee and Roger entertained us and we played card games. Later, Roger showed us how to tie the best fishing knots. He said money can buy a lot of things, but a man has to know how to tie good knots and that can't be purchased. Roger also told us that a good knot keeps a man fishing longer and retying less. We learned to tie four kinds of knots: the best terminal knots, line-to-line splices, light-to-heavy line splices, and terminal loop knots.

Dad and Melvin are really tired tonight. Uncle Melvin promised us that tomorrow we'll have some fun and go fishing. Easton and I are excited to tie our own knots. Maybe Dee Dee and Roger will go with us. I really like them. They remind me of Nana and Papa Alfred.

Dear Summer,

Something vandalized Dad's truck last night! Uncle Melvin left the window down when he took us to the lake store to get a soda and more gum. It looks like something off of a horror movie. The seats were sliced up, the dash was chewed, and the knobs to the stereo were torn completely off. The vandal also managed to get into my stash of bubble gum. All of the packages were opened and some of the pieces were gone. It left tracks in the front seat and pooped in the back seat. My dad always keeps his truck clean. He washes it almost every Saturday. He was furious! I don't think I've ever seen my dad that mad. Uncle Melvin apologized and said he would help him repair the truck. Dad said it was okay, but I know he didn't mean it! Dad is trying really hard to move on and forget about it, but I can tell he just wants to scream.

Tonight we have a plan. We're going to stay up and find out what tore up Dad's truck. Uncle Melvin said we would use the truck as bait since it's already messed up. Dad was up for it. He wanted to teach a lesson to whatever did this! I can see it in his eyes. Dad is ready to get even.

Dear Summer,

As promised, we went fishing. The only knot I could remember was a terminal loop knot. Dad was pretty impressed I could tie such a mean knot. We caught some good sized bass and a couple of catfish. Uncle Melvin kept them and cleaned them. We had fresh fish for dinner. Uncle Melvin learned how to cook at the fire station. I guess the firemen have to take turns cooking. Dad went to the lake store and bought us some potato salad at the deli. For a bunch of guys, we did a good job. Even Dee Dee and Roger came over. Dee Dee made hushpuppies, and Roger brought his stomach. Lizzy and Jet enjoyed the leftovers.

Tonight we are hoping to find out what shredded Dad's truck. I sure hope it isn't a bear or some type of wolf. That would be scary if things like that are running around the campsite at night. If so, I'll never come camping again. Wish us luck!

Dear Tired Summer,

We stayed up almost all night trying to find out what destroyed Dad's truck. After we ate dinner, Uncle Melvin pulled us together for a team meeting. He said we had to work quickly so that we could be ready. He really got excited! I can sure tell country dads are different than

city dads. My dad would've just called someone about prices to repair the truck, but Uncle Melvin wanted to capture the villain.

Easton and I were put in charge of gathering tree limbs and brush so we could create our own hideout. Uncle Melvin said that in order to watch, we had to camouflage ourselves on the porch in a comfortable position. We both walked the camping area trying to find the best mini branches. Dee Dee and Roger had fun helping us get our blinds ready. Dee Dee even painted our faces with some mud she gathered. Dee Dee and Roger kept Lizzy and Jet for the night to keep them from barking.

Dad was in charge of finding some food to leave in his truck. Since the truck was already messed up, Dad figured we should lure them back. Dad was still mad and just wanted to see the critter face to face. Uncle Melvin went to find a big piece of plywood about the size of Dad's window.

Dad gathered all of the food he planned on using as bait. Uncle Melvin dug in the storage shed behind the cabin. He found a large piece of plywood they must have used to board up a window because it had nail holes all around it. (At least that is what Uncle Melvin said.) We all helped Uncle Melvin tie the board to the truck so the bottom of the board was even with the bottom of the truck window. Uncle Melvin drilled larger holes in each of the corners so we could tie rope into both top corners. He ran the rope around to the other side of the truck. The plan was for all of us (except Uncle Melvin) to wait on the porch. Uncle Melvin had the dangerous job of holding

the ropes steady just on the other side of the truck while being covered with a tarp. He was in charge of the "lid" we made for the window. Dad's second job was to send a signal to Uncle Melvin by flashing his light at him when the critter entered the truck window to get the food. Uncle Melvin would then pull the plywood window shut and anchor it down so we could see what was tearing up Dad's truck. SIMPLE PLAN!

Things sort of worked out the way we planned. Dee Dee helped us get covered up in tree limbs and shrubs. She used lots of rope. Dad put on some of Uncle Melvin's hunting clothes he had in the back of his truck, and Melvin didn't need anything because he was going to be covered in a tarp. Once it got dark, we all got into our assigned spots. Easton and I had a hard time being quiet, but we heard something that sounded like a low growl and scratch on top of the cabin porch. That scared us into being quiet. All of a sudden, we heard something jump on top of Dad's truck. It was about the size of a small monkey. Then another one jumped off the cabin roof and onto the truck. After that I'm not sure how many more came to join in, but it was a lot. They scurried all over the outside of the truck making scratching noises. Dad had a bag of garbage in the back of the truck that we had forgotten about, and they all got inside of the garbage sack and took out everything and began eating our leftovers. One of them grabbed an empty box of cereal from our garbage bag and pulled it inside the truck. It was an amazing thing to see! Then, all of the others followed and started going crazy over the

food Dad left in the truck. They were making a growling noise and really going after it! I'd never heard those sounds before. Dad flashed the light at Uncle Melvin and triggered Uncle Melvin to pull the ropes so the plywood blocked the window. Uncle Melvin tied the ropes down so the critters couldn't get out. Dad turned on the cabin porch light, and we all ran to the truck window to see what it was that we had captured.

Raccoons! We captured a bunch of raccoons. There were lots of babies too, and they were hungry. Once they realized they were trapped, the critters started to get mad. One even opened Dad's glove box and began throwing things everywhere. Dad shined the light in the truck, and they started going crazy! They didn't like the light! One of them even hit the window with its paw. Dad went nuts because all he could see was his truck getting destroyed. He was planning on one critter, not an entire family critter reunion!

Uncle Melvin knew the wildlife ranger in the area so he called him immediately to ask what we should do. The ranger told him there wasn't anything they could do and to let them go. He said that keeping them locked up was dangerous, and that they've had lots of problems lately because the area was overpopulated.

After getting off the phone, Uncle Melvin announced that we had to let them go. He made Easton and me get in the cabin. He didn't want us getting hurt. So we watched through the window. Melvin and Dad released the plywood trap door and the raccoons raced out. Once the coast was clear, Dad ran to his truck and opened the

door to see the damage done to his beloved truck. There was one problem. All of the critters hadn't gotten out! There was still one little feller left in the back cab. He was feasting on a piece of catfish. I guess Dad startled him, because he jumped at Dad and used him as a tree to climb out. Dad started screaming and running around in circles. Uncle Melvin ran towards Dad and checked him. Dad kept yelling, "Get it off! Get it off!" Uncle Melvin was yelling for him to stay still. Dee Dee and Roger must have heard, because they came running over. Dee Dee took Dad in the cabin. He was scratched up and bleeding all over his face. I was so scared. His shirt was sliced like someone had taken a knife to it. Dee Dee started cleaning him up. Dad was shaking!

Uncle Melvin took Dad to the hospital and Dee Dee stayed with us at the cabin. She promised us we would be safe and the raccoons wouldn't get near us. She said critters like that are meant to be left alone and are used to doing things their way. When humans interrupt their normal life, it makes them upset.

I haven't seen Dad yet. I peeked outside my window and Uncle Melvin's truck is parked outside the cabin. I know they are back. I'm sure they are tired, so I'm just going to leave them alone. I hope Dad is okay. If Mom was here, she would've protected Dad and Melvin from their ideas. We probably would've made Smores or told stories by a campfire. We wouldn't have tried to trap critters. I sure didn't think it was a bad idea at the time and neither did Dad.

Dear Raccoon Summer,

Dad's face is covered in scratches and cuts. Apparently raccoons have razor like nails. Uncle Melvin said bandit-masked raccoons are very thick in this area. The doctor told them last night that raccoons carry lots of diseases and one of the worst is parasite-borne and known as raccoon roundworm. The doctor said it could cause blindness and even death in humans. Uncle Melvin said the doctor gave Dad some shots and thought he would be okay since he wasn't bitten. They washed all of the wounds out and cleaned him up.

I'm positive that camping isn't going to be one of Dad's favorite things to do anymore. After hearing about all of the diseases raccoons carry, Dad has decided it's time for a new truck. It looks worse now than it did before. I don't blame Dad for not wanting it anymore. Roger told Dad there is someone in town who buys used cars and trucks. Roger is going to drop by and talk to the man for him. I guess Dad doesn't even want to drive it back home. That's probably a good idea since the interior is shredded and covered with raccoon poop! What makes things worse is that Dad just paid off his truck last year. Every time we get in it, he reminds me that cars and trucks ride better when you drive them for free.

Dear Bummer Summer,

When I woke up, Dad was preparing breakfast. He said Mom and Aunt Jamie were on their way! They missed us and were finished shopping. We still had three more days of camp host life. I asked him if he told Mom what happened and he said he didn't. Boy is Mom going to be crazy about this! I'm not sure what he was thinking. First she is going to see Dad's face and panic, and then she is going to get a look at the truck and start crying. She'll probably think we were involved in some sort of horrific accident. This time, I had nothing to do with it! Dad and Uncle Melvin are going to have a lot of explaining to do!

Dear Tear Your Face Off By a Raccoon Summer,

They're here and they showed up with my cousin Angela! Mom flipped! I thought the firework "experience" had rendered her speechless, but I was wrong. She saw Dad with bandages covering his face and began checking him from head to toe. Aunt Jamie immediately ran to Uncle Melvin and Easton to check on them. Mom

looked at me and then focused on Dad. She had all of the typical questions you'd expect your mom to ask when your dad looks like he was mangled. After about an hour of questions, Dad showed Mom the truck. She started laughing! I expected her to scream, yell, or cry and she laughed. She couldn't quit laughing. Shopping must have made her lose her mind. Dad looks like he's the walking dead and she's laughing at the truck. To make things seem even odder, Aunt Jamie and Angela started laughing too. Soon, everyone was laughing!

This reaction made my dad and Uncle Melvin flip into silly comedian mode. They began to retell the story, and boy did they exaggerate! Easton and I kept laughing because we knew what really happened. Dad and Uncle Melvin acted out the chain of events. Dee Dee and Roger heard all of the laughter and came over. Mom thanked Dee Dee for taking care of us. Mom mentioned the apple thing to Dee Dee. I asked Mom what that meant and she said that Dad and I were a lot alike and we came from the same tree. Everyone laughed again!

Dear Summer,

It's been a very long week. Today is our last day as camp hosts and we will leave in the morning. Dad and Roger took the truck to an old car lot in town and they bought it for $4,000. The man said it looked like a great truck

and all it needed was new seats. Dad was glad to have the truck gone. He seems excited to get a new one. Mom said he deserved it after what he's been through this summer.

Our cousin Angela is a little older. She is in 8th grade. Dad let her drive us around on the golf cart today. We took firewood to the campers who requested it and collected firewood from campsites that had been vacated. We also had to clean out the fire pits. Sometimes people try to burn cans and other things so we had to scoop out all the trash that didn't burn. Lizzy and Jet came with us. They like riding in the golf cart.

Tonight we got to see the firework display. Dad enjoyed watching it from a distance. We both jumped at the first sound of fireworks. Towards the end of the show, Angela drove us down to the bank so we could watch the finale near the water. She even showed us how to skip rocks across the lake. She's really good at rock skipping and could make a rock skip up to four times.

I kind of don't want to leave this place. I'm glad that Uncle Melvin asked us to come along and help. We definitely made a lot of memories. Tonight we all sat out around the campfire and Mom helped us make Smores. Dee Dee and Roger joined us. They are kind of like family now. Roger told stories about Vietnam. I'm sure going to miss them. I heard Mom and Dad giving

116

Dee Dee and Roger our address and then told them to come see us sometime. Roger could show all of my friends how to tie those cool fishing knots!

Dear Summer,

We just pulled away from the cabin and are on the road headed home. Aunt Jamie rode back home with Uncle Melvin and Easton. Dad and I are riding back with Mom and Angela since our truck didn't survive the trip. Uncle Melvin is taking back all of our big stuff and Dad said we will get it next time we are at the farm. It wouldn't fit in Mom's car. Angela, Dad and Lizzy are already asleep. Angela passes out anytime she rides in a car, and Dad is just worn out. As for Lizzy, she's just a normal dog. I might try to take a nap also.

I kind of like being from the same tree as my dad. He'll do anything for me. I know that camping isn't his thing, but he did it all for me. Sometimes we just do things for people because we love them. He's a pretty good dad. I think I like sharing apples with him, and I am glad we are from the same tree!

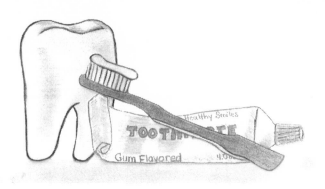

Chapter Nine

Mad Gum Disease

Dear Itchy Summer,

I woke up this morning with a REALLY bad itch. My arms and face are covered in a rash! Mom took one look at me and became hysterical. She couldn't figure out what caused it, and Dad remembered Dee Dee covered me in the tree branches I collected. Mom is taking me to the doctor later. She thinks I was in contact with poison ivy. POISON IVY sounds poisonous! I hope I don't die! This ITCHES!

Dear Scratchy Summer,

I want to SCRATCH! Mom said to focus on something that would take my mind off of the urge to scratch, so I thought I'd write about the urge to scratch. All I can think about is itching! I need to SCRATCH! I need to ITCH! I need to SCRATCH!

Dear Bummer Summer,

It's confirmed! I'm allergic to poison ivy! Mom called Dee Dee and she broke out on her arms too. Easton didn't break out for some reason. Lucky Easton!

Dear Itchy-Scratchy-Stinky-Miserable-Summer,

The doctor said I would be fine in a week or two. Two weeks sounds like a lifetime when you have to itch this bad! Mom is trying everything she can to make me comfortable, but it isn't working. Everyone keeps telling me to NOT ITCH! NOT ITCH? That's impossible. Why do adults tell you not to itch when you want to peel your skin like a banana? I'm trying really hard, but this stinks—big time!

Instead of itching, I'm slapping the itch spot. That helps some, but I look stupid walking around the house slapping myself. When I do it, everyone laughs. Dad said I look like I'm at war with myself.

I miss my friends. I can't go visit them while I'm all broke out. Mom keeps putting this pink lotion on my skin, so I look silly. I hope none of my friends come to the door. I look like I've been dipped in pink cotton candy!

Dear Bummer Summer,

Mom read on the Internet that blow-drying your skin makes you quit wanting to itch, so about every hour Mom blow-dries my skin. It actually helps! I also took a bath in water with baking soda. It's starting to let up just a little bit. I sleep a lot!

Dear Summer,

The skin is feeling a lot better now. The rash is beginning to look better. Mom said she was surprised at how fast I'm healing. I guess my skin is ready to see my friends too. Dad said we get to go to Mexico in two weeks. I'm so excited! To pass the time in solitary confinement, I've been looking at pictures of where we'll be staying.

Dear Summer,

Finally, I got to play with Jimmy and Matthew. Mom didn't let me stay out too long because she didn't want to make my rash mad. It's been an uneventful day. Kind of nice!

Dear Pickled Summer,

My dill pickle flavored bubble gum arrived today! It tasted just like dill pickles. I shared it with all my friends. Sam acted like he was puking, and Maddie said it tasted really bad. Everyone else seemed to think it was good. I guess you have to like pickles.

Dear Summer,

Erin and Logan invited me to play on the trampoline. Logan is Erin's little brother. He is four. I have a black Spiderman he loves to play with, so when he sees me he asks for black Spiderman. I took it to him to play with and he ran around the yard pretending he was black Spiderman. We laughed!

Dear Not-So-Great Summer,

First poison ivy and now this! I have a tooth that aches really bad. When am I going to catch a break? Mom made me a dental appointment. What if they have to cut this

part of my mouth out? I've never had a tooth pulled at the dentist office, and I'm not sure I want to start now. Maybe I should just run away! Maybe I should tell them it doesn't hurt anymore. Maybe I should just lie down. I think the pain meds Mom gave me are starting to kick in now.

Dear Achy Summer,

MY MOUTH HAS A HEARTBEAT! It is pounding with pain.

Dear Summer,

Now I have the start of some mouth disease! I don't remember exactly what the dentist said, but Mom called it Mad Gum Disease. That sounds terrible. I hope I don't die. I'm feeling really crummy. I have to go back to the dentist in two days for a special cleaning. Good news is they didn't have to cut on my mouth. Bad news is that I have Mad Gum Disease.

Dear Summer,

I looked up Mad Gum Disease on the Internet and there is nothing out there. This must be something new. What if I am the first person to have such a disease? I hope I pull through this one.

Dear Summer,

I went back to the dentist. As soon as I got there I caved. I asked them if I was going to die, and they all laughed. What is it with people laughing lately? I asked them if Mad Gum Disease killed people because I couldn't find anything about it on the Internet. The dental hygienist laughed and said there was no such thing. Immediately I looked at my mom. She said, "GOTCHA!" I didn't think it was very funny.

Gum = 1, Mom = 2

I did have an infection in my gums around my tooth. If I didn't get it taken care of now, it would've turned into periodontal disease. Mom guessed it was probably due to the fact that I chew way too much gum. The hygienist didn't disagree.

Boy did that cleaning hurt! It felt like someone was sand blasting my gums. Then they took this sharp object and scraped along my gum line. It was painful! I might lay off the gum a little bit. I don't want to have this done EVER AGAIN!

Chapter Ten

Mexico!

Dear Summer,

It's been a while since I've written you. Between the rash and toothache I've been trying to play catch up with my friends. School starts in two weeks. I can't believe summer break is almost over. Where did it go?

Tomorrow we leave for Mexico. I'm kind of nervous. Mom is running around with her checklist like Mrs. Magle on the last day of school. She's packing everything for us. Mom told Dad she really needed a relaxing vacation before school started back up. Hopefully she gets her wish because Dad has put a lot of stress on her with the way he's been acting lately.

Dear Mexican Summer,

I'm waiting in the airport. Grandma Jo dropped us off really early this morning. Mom has gone overboard with the vacation thing. She's wearing a big floppy hat and lots of red lipstick. I asked Dad if she was trying to scare the other passengers, and Dad grinned and told me to not say that out loud again. I know he's thinking the same thing. He's just afraid to admit his thoughts.

There are a lot of strange looking people at the airport. We are in terminal number 2 waiting for our boarding instructions. It will be about an hour before we board the plane. Across from me is a woman with twin babies traveling by herself. She seems scared. I'd be scared too if I was traveling alone. Mom spotted the babies right away and started to talk to her. She keeps telling her how cute the babies are and is asking all sorts of questions. I know she just wants to hold them. Mom likes babies! She says she doesn't, but people who don't like babies stay away from babies. My mom is like a bug to a light when it comes to babies. I think babies look like little old men. They sort of creep me out!

Dear Summer,

We've boarded the plane. Mom helped the lady with the babies and is actually sitting by the baby machine and the two babies. Dad and I are towards the back of the plane. It's best to sit in the back of the plane because if you have to go to the bathroom, then you don't have to go very far. Plus, if Mom makes one of the babies cry, then we won't be near all of the crying. Crying babies make Dad nervous! Mom on the other hand, gets loud and starts telling the baby all the reasons it shouldn't cry. Most of the time, the baby will stop crying. I'm guessing it's probably because they are tired of listening to her.

Dear Summer,

We completed the first flight, laid over in Houston, Texas, ate at the airport, and are currently in the air on our connecting flight. We will be in Cozumel, Mexico in about 45 minutes according to the pilot. Dad is asleep and is starting to snore. His raccoon scratches are beginning to heal, but people still look at the poor guy like he was beaten up or in a bad car accident. Each time he tells the story, it expands. I just sit back and laugh. My dad is known for his ability to tell a funny story.

Mom did okay with the babies. Dad had to make her leave the babies alone in Houston and boy was I glad

those babies were staying and not going to Cozumel! Mom had both of them covered in red lipstick by the end of the flight. I hope they aren't allergic to red lipstick! Mom is sitting beside me reading travel brochures and is planning what we'll do as soon as we arrive. To pass the time, we made a list of what would be gross bubble gum flavors. I'll have to share these with my friend Austin. He likes bubble gum too, and I'd like to know if he would try any of them. Maybe he would if I TRIPLE DOG DARED him WITH NO TAKE BACKS.

Top Ten Grossest Bubble Gum Flavors:

1. Poison Ivy
2. Baby Poo
3. Lizard
4. Broccoli
5. Black Tar
6. Raccoon (This one was for Dad)
7. Swimming Pool
8. Fish
9. Vinegar
10. Sweat

Yeah, we are about to land! I have to put everything away. Mexico, here comes Gum!

Dear Summer,

What a day! As soon as we got off of the plane, we saw military men with guns and big dogs. At first I was scared, but Mom said they were part of the airport security. As we entered the building, I saw a soldier playing with one of the dogs and then the dog started smelling all of our luggage as it came off of the plane. I was hoping it wouldn't pee on my luggage because I have a week's worth of gum in my bag.

I gave someone my passport and got my very first stamp in my book! The man didn't say a word, and he was really fast. I thought he would for sure say something about not smiling in my photo, but he didn't. The line was really long. Mom visited with everyone in line and shared our schedule. She found a couple who had never been here before, so she told them everything she knew. I think they were glad when it was their turn at the counter.

After we found our luggage, we walked outside again and people with clipboards ran towards us and told us we were supposed to come with them. Dad grabbed me and looked for our travel guide. Jose greeted us and pulled us from the crowd. Then, this little short man grabbed our bags and put them in a van loaded with people. I've never been to Mexico, but everything happened fast and the little man was really nice. The shuttle ride to our hotel was scary! The driver didn't speak much English, and he never stopped at a stop sign. He just honked his horn. While driving down the main street, he honked

at people in his way, drove up on the sidewalk with the van, and zipped around obstacles. Once we all thought we were going to crash into pedestrians, but we didn't. Dad sat in the front seat of the van and noticed others were stressed about the drive. Everyone in the van spoke English, so Dad told them all about getting attacked by a raccoon. People started to relax. The driver looked at Dad like he was crazy. He started driving even faster. Mom whispered to me and told me she thought the driver was ready to get rid of Dad. Our resort was on the very end of the island, so we were the last family to be dropped off. As the driver took our luggage out of the van, he handed Dad his bag and said "Raccoon Man". Dad laughed and gave him money. I guess Dad really liked the new name, and I guess the driver understood most of Dad's story after all.

The resort we are staying at is really nice. There are several swimming pools and palm trees are everywhere. We're in the middle of a jungle. I said it, a jungle!

Right now Mom and Dad are unpacking. They told me to sit on the deck and look around, but I thought I'd write about our adventure to the resort from the airport. There really isn't much to see from our room. I see lots of trees and leaves bigger than my body. This place is hot and sticky!

Dear Miserable Summer,

Oh man! Mom and Dad are furious. Our air conditioner in our room doesn't work. It's so hot here. Because the resort is in the middle of a jungle, there is no breeze. We went to the pool by our room today after putting our things away and the pool was like a hot tub. The pool was actually hotter than the air. I still haven't seen the ocean since we've been here. I saw it when the shuttle driver was driving, so I know it's around here somewhere. Guess I'll try to find it tomorrow.

Right now Dad is gone. He went to find our check in person to tell her about the air conditioning. Mom and I are lying on our beds and being real still. We both have towels and are trying to soak up the sweat as it pours from our bodies. So far this trip isn't what I thought it would be like.

Dear Summer,

Someone came back to our room with Dad. They walked in and said, "We get you new room!" They moved us to a room below and it was much cooler. Mom started getting happier almost immediately. We all took cold showers and are watching television. All of the channels are in Spanish. It's kind of cool to see SpongeBob speaking Spanish. I didn't know the television would be in Spanish too. Good night Mexico!

Dear Summer,

We all slept fine on our hard beds. We were so tired that I don't think it mattered. Dad says breakfast should be good, so we are about to head down to get some omelets made to order. We are waiting on Mom to put on her red lipstick and floppy hat. I AM HUNGRY!

Dear Summer,

What a day! Where do I begin? Breakfast was great. Dad tipped the woman making the omelets, and she went to the back and grabbed some additional toppings for our omelets. She showed them to Dad and he nodded his head. Then she just started adding lots of things to our food. I can tell Dad has done this before. He takes breakfast seriously.

After breakfast, we were walking back to our room to change into our swimsuits and Mom tripped and fell. When we looked back, she had a huge iguana about four feet long standing next to her. It was brown and bright orange. The iguana just stared at her as she screamed. Someone from the resort came to her assistance almost immediately and introduced us to the iguana. His name

was "Speedy". Dad and I were stunned, we couldn't help her. I guess we were waiting to see if it was going to eat her face. She wasn't real happy that we didn't rescue her, but neither of us had seen anyone trip on an iguana before. It just ran out in front of her and neither of us saw it. Maybe that's how he got his name "Speedy".

After we changed into our swimsuits, we went to meet a guide who showed us around the property. We met him at breakfast. Mom and Dad were asking lots of "location" questions, so he said he would just take us around the resort and show us the sights. He was originally from Australia and had a cool accent. He kept calling me "mate". It sounded funny! We spotted the kids club, all the restaurants, the pools, and then he walked us across this long wooden bridge through the trees. At first I thought he was taking us to some secret place, but then the trees cleared and all I could see was sand, huts, boats, and the ocean. This is what I had waited for and I had finally found it! There's also a restaurant by the ocean. Lunch is served daily right on the shore.

Our guide left us since he had shown us everything we needed to see. Mom and I jumped in the pool and as soon as we did, my mom asked a woman what time it was and she instantly found new friends. Geno and Amanda were nice. They are on their honeymoon and are here from Kansas. Amanda visited with Mom, and I started practicing with my new snorkel set. Dad went back to the front desk to arrange a snorkel trip for us later in the day. He said I need to experience the reefs.

I'm not sure what a reef is, but Mom said it's definitely something I should experience.

After about an hour, Mom had not only one couple, but two couples she had pulled into her new circle of friends. I was glad because the second set of friends had a boy that was really nice. His name is Cody. They just got to the resort also and are here from Northern California.

When Dad got back from booking our snorkeling trip, he noticed Mom was busy with lots of friends, so we played ping pong by the pool. My dad is a ping pong champion! Mom said Dad spent more of his time in college playing ping pong than studying.

Later we had lunch by the ocean with all of our new friends. After lunch we walked to the pier and waited for a glass bottom boat to come and get us to go snorkeling. I thought it would be a lot like snorkeling in the swimming pool, but boy was I wrong! The water was bright blue, almost turquoise. The first place we stopped was an area loaded with starfish. Everywhere you looked, you saw starfish! The water took some getting used to because it was so salty. One big mouthful of saltwater and you learn to keep your mouth shut. The second place they took us was on top of a big reef full of colorful fish and plants. We spotted a lobster and some stingrays too! By the time we got to the last place, I was tired. We were lucky because we got to see a really big sea turtle in the water. It was huge and looked really old. Sea turtles can live a long time. I was so impressed by the sea turtles that I swallowed a big gulp of ocean water and instantly felt like I was going to hurl! Thankfully I didn't, but I still feel sick.

We spent the rest of the night swimming in the pool visiting with our new friends. Cody and I practiced our snorkeling and played football. Geno also showed us a tree that was full of bananas. Cody and I are thinking of a way we can get those bananas down, but the area looks very sharp and pokey!

I have to get some rest. I still feel like I need to puke up some salt. Maybe I'll feel better in the morning. Dad is snoring in his bed and Mom is trying to text Grandma Jo to tell her that we are all ok.

Dear Coconut Summer,

Today we jumped in a rental jeep with Cody's family and explored the back side of the island. It was awesome! Not a lot of people live on that side of the island because it's the side that gets hit the most with hurricanes. We were supposed to go meet up with some people to help dig baby sea turtles out of the sand, but the timing wasn't perfect so we looked at the turtle tracks instead. Mom was able to throw flowers in the ocean for Nana, Papa Alfred, and Papa John. She cried a little bit, so I told her that I would put flowers in the ocean for her when she dies. She said it was sweet of me, but she didn't plan on leaving anytime soon. That made me feel good because I sort of like my mom!

Cody's step dad is a fireman like Uncle Melvin and

acts a lot like him too. When we were driving, Cody's step dad stopped the jeep and jumped out because he saw a coconut. He banged it against a rock until it opened, but it was rotten.

We stopped at a few other places to watch waves crash into the big rocks. I'm glad we went. I found a coconut of my own and tried to crack it, but it wouldn't crack.

Dear Summer,

After breakfast today, Dad announced we are going swimming at a stingray beach. I really am not sure how I feel about swimming with animals that could cause a person harm. Right now Dad is calling the front desk for a taxi so we can go. I may not make it back alive! I don't know why my parents continue to put me in situations that are so dangerous. Ugh, PARENTS THESE DAYS!

Dear Stingray Attack Summer,

Although it was cool, I doubt I'll want to do that again for a long time. The stingray adventure was divided into three parts. During the first part, we snorkeled with a lot

of stingrays while a man fed them down below. I guess the biggest one there thought I was her friend because she found me and kept gliding under my belly. The guide said she liked me. (We knew it was a female because the small stingrays are male and the big stingrays are female.)

Then, we went to the learning section of the beach and learned all about stingrays. We held them, and I learned about their barbs. All of the barbs on these stingrays had been clipped off so they couldn't harm us. We held two stingrays. They were like puppies. I also didn't know people actually ate stingrays. It was very interesting, but it also grossed me out at the same time.

Finally, we were at the last section of the beach where we were supposed to "interact" with the rays. A man showed me how to feed them and then loaded me up with small fish. I was scared because there were lots of stingrays circling me. They were like sharks circling before an attack. Mom and Dad stepped back and kept laughing. I didn't think it was very funny! I put one fish under the water and the rays rushed to get to it and about knocked me over. Then it happened! A gigantic female stingray, that must have been super hungry, got a running start at me and darted into my feet. She bulldozed me down and caused me to drop all of my fish. They all started towards me and suddenly I was covered in stingrays. They weren't after me, but at the time I didn't know it. My heart was about to pound out of my chest. I fell and landed on top of one of them and all

of them started flopping and flapping in the water as if they hadn't eaten in decades! Dad jumped to my rescue and Mom started screaming for the guide to come save me. As soon as I got back on my feet, I bolted for the shore. My hand was cut up, and my knee was bleeding. I had enough of the stingray adventure! I'm still not sure why people would pay for an experience where you get attacked by dangerous animals, but my parents took the bait. They knew I wasn't happy.

Afterwards, I was pretty shaken so my parents took me to an area where we enjoyed a snack and dried off. Then, we took a cab further into town so we could do some shopping. I learned how to negotiate with the shop owners. I bought some shirts, bracelets, and maracas for my friends back home. Mom bought some stuff for her classroom, and Dad found some gifts for their friends. Most of the shops were full of the same things, so shopping didn't last long. Mom found herself a bright red floppy hat. Now she has two!

When we arrived back at the resort, Mom took me to the English speaking doctor and he bandaged up my hand and knee. I wasn't real happy with the doctor. Mom told him all about the incident and they both began acting it out like I wasn't even there. I was happy when the visit ended.

After visiting with our new friends, we went to change into some nice clothes. Dad had made reservations to eat at a steak house on the resort. That meant I had to shower, wear dress pants, and a collared shirt with

some nice shoes. I was kind of hoping Mom would run into Speedy again. That was funny!

Now I get to meet up with Cody to go swimming in the big pool. I can't wait! He went to see the fire show, so I have to ask him all about it.

Dear Summer,

We woke up and it's raining. Not just a little bit of rain either! It's pouring down rain. We want to go to breakfast, but we heard a very loud whistle and figured it meant we needed to stay indoors. I'm hungry! As soon as it quits, we'll go eat breakfast. I hope Dad tips the cook again. The omelets are really good here. Mom enjoys the papaya and potatoes. I won't try papaya because it sounds funny.

Dad is watching television and is trying to repeat the Spanish phrases. Mom is looking at a flyer on the Mayan Ruins. I think she wants to go. It sounds fun. I'm about to go downstairs and see if the cat is hanging out. The housekeeper said his name was Pedro. He's a very lazy cat. He likes me. Mom is allergic to cats, so she can't pet Pedro.

Gum = 2, Mom = 2

Dear Sandy Summer,

After the rain stopped, we went to breakfast and then laid around the resort. Later, our new friends talked us into walking the beach to a seafood restaurant. Cody went also. Mom gave both of us a small bag so we could collect shells along the way. It was great! The restaurant was outside with tables on the beach. While the adults sat and talked about adults stuff, Cody joined me in a seashell hunt. We found shells bigger than our heads. They were heavy! There were lots of shells washing up on the beach. We played for a really long time until the music started. Then we went back up on the beach and danced while the band played fun songs. We walked back in the dark. No one brought a light, so it was kind of scary. Tonight was fun, just me and my new friend. Oh, and lots and lots of sand and seashells!

Dear Mayan Summer,

All of our friends want to go see the Mayan Ruins with us. Mom hasn't stopped talking about it, so everyone decided today is the day to go see them. Apparently there are a lot of people from the resort going. I brought my journal because Mom said it's about three hours from Cozumel, and we have to get on a passenger ferry to get to the mainland. We have two vans full of people,

and it's still dark outside. This driver is not as scary as the last driver.

Dear Ferry Boat Summer,

The vans dropped us off at the main port in town and now we are taking a ferry to a place called Playa del Carmen. Once we get there, we will be taken to a Mayan Ruin called Chichen Itza. It sounds fun, but I'm so tired. I can smell the salt off of the ocean. I've decided that the ocean never gets tired.

Dear Summer,

I fell asleep on the ferry and now we are in a big van. Cody is in the other van with his parents. I think I'll go to sleep. Chichen Itza is one of the Seven Wonders of the World, but I'm wondering why people go see it. It sure is a long way from our resort. We were told to get comfortable because we have to drive over 100 miles to get there. I don't think I'm too big to take a nap in my mom's lap. That actually sounds good right now! I'm so sleepy.

Dear Horrible Summer,

MY MOM IS GONE! We don't know where she is and have no idea how to get a hold of her. We didn't bring cell phones because the coverage is bad. OH NO!

Dear Summer,

Dad put me back on the ferry with Cody's family. He found a taxi driver and is headed back to Chichen Itza. The best we can figure is Mom didn't make it back on a shuttle van. I hope he finds my mom! We were so tired; we just thought she was on the other shuttle van. I wish I could have gone with Dad to find Mom. This is just terrible!

Dear Summer,

I'm back at the resort. Cody's family has a room right next to ours and Dad gave them our room key. Cody's mom is staying with me until they get back. She's really nice and ordered room service. I don't feel like eating though. I really want my mom! What if something happens to my dad too?

Dear Summer with NO PARENTS,

I just woke up and still don't have my parents. I haven't heard from them and now I don't have my mom or my dad. I sure hope they are okay. I think I kind of know what Mom and Dad felt like when they lost Nana, Papa Alfred, and Papa John. I should've stayed with Mom. She needs someone to watch her. She wanted to go explore on her own, so we let her. We should've stayed with her.

Dear Summer,

Cody's mom just told me that my parents contacted the resort and they are both fine and on their way home. They had to stay at a hotel in Playa for the night because the ferry boat had shut down for the night. That's all I know, but that's all I need to know. I never want to lose them again! From now on, I'll watch them and keep a better eye on them. They'll be here in a couple of hours.

Dear Summer,

Mom and Dad are here! They both made it safely. Mom cried when she saw me and I think I cried too! I never want to think about not having my parents ever again.

Dear Summer,

After all of the excitement, we spent the day just lying around on the beach with our new friends. Cody and his step dad went snorkeling with us, and we saw a lionfish! It was really cool. Cody's step dad said lionfish were very dangerous. That might be something else I need to read more about.

We go home tomorrow, and I'm kind of glad. I want to get my parents back home where they'll be safe. Mom is still a little nervous and shaken. She said she would tell me all about it when we get home.

Dear Summer,

I think I've had enough adventure for one week. We are at the airport. Mom isn't wearing a big floppy hat, and she isn't wearing her red lipstick. She and Dad are just

sitting beside each other holding hands. I think she's scared to leave his side. I hope she tells me everything.

Dear Summer,

Our flight to Houston, Texas was fine. However, we just got on the plane in Houston after going through immigration and we realized we left my backpack at the airport. It was full of our souvenirs. I also had my wallet in the bag. I hope someone finds it and turns it in to lost and found.

Dear Summer,

We are home, and I wish I had my bag. I'm ready to give my friends all of the gifts I had picked up during our trip.

Dear Summer of Good News,

Good news! We left our bag at a baggage checkpoint at the airport. Mom and Dad were still so shaken from the Mayan incident that they just walked off and left it.

Mom called the lost and found at the airport and they did have a bag matching the description. Mom then had to list all of the items in the bag and I guess they were such strange things that the person in lost and found told her it was for sure our bag. They are going to ship our bag back to us!

Dear Summer,

Today Dad went back to work and we just hung out around the house. Mom told me all about what happened in Mexico. She said she got so caught up in what she was seeing that she didn't check her watch to see when she was supposed to load up in the van to go back to the resort. We are so used to her finding other people to talk to that we didn't think anything about her not being on our van. We just thought she was riding back with someone else so she could talk more. Mom had never been left behind. She's a schedule queen.

The Mayan Ruins closed at 5 p.m. and Mom noticed people leaving. She then looked at her watch and started to freak. She was smart because she found someone that spoke English and they waited with her. She knew Dad would show up to get her once he realized she wasn't on the van. The cab ride cost them $264 U.S. dollars, but Mom said she was worth the expense.

Mom was really scared at first, but she knew nothing

would tear our family apart. She promised to never wander off and to always let us know where she was going, and I promised I would do the same. From now on, we will always ride together, but I'm sure it will be a while before we take another tour.

Dear Bummer Summer,

This is my last entry. I only have a few days left before school starts back up. Mom said I didn't have to write in my journal anymore, and that I needed to enjoy my last few days of freedom. It actually made me kind of sad. I started my summer mad because of the writing assignment, but now I have a journal that will let me remember every bit of my amazing summer. I hope Mrs. Magle enjoyed her summer too. If we get asked about our favorite part of summer, I will say my favorite part was my family. Family is most important! My family may be strange, but we love each other.

Epilogue

Dear Gum,

Your writer's notebook is very interesting! I especially liked the part about how your teacher and mother were potential alien threats. I am sorry the police got called. I was startled when I saw someone looking through my window. Seems you were convinced you were in the company of extraterrestrial visitors from another planet.

Jimmy's birthday was fun. I enjoyed myself at the party. We need to consider having Dan's Animal Kingdom visit our school. Would you lead a fundraiser so we could pay for it? My dog needs a bath? (Ha, Ha)

I am sorry you had to spend several days working on shutting down your grandparent's farm. I know you loved going there and spending time with them. It does sound like your Uncle Melvin and Aunt Jamie will keep you busy with more adventures on their farm. Your cousin Easton sounds a lot like you. I can only imagine what kind of trouble the two of you can conjure up.

I hope your dad is okay from your adventure as "camp hosts". It really sounds like he took a beating! I saw some

scratches on his face, but didn't want to ask about them. Your dad is nice. He helped me the other day when I was working in the yard. Remind me to NEVER go camping with your family! Dee Dee and Roger sound really nice too. If they visit, do you think they would consider visiting our classroom? I bet they have lots of interesting stories to tell!

Your Mom still seems a little worn out from the vacation. She hasn't told me much about it, but I know she will when she's ready. I hope she will travel again. She loves to travel, and I would sure hate to have something like this cause her to quit traveling. Maybe we shouldn't study the Mayan Ruins this year!

You did an amazing job writing. I am very proud of you. You wrote more than I expected and went above and beyond. You are an author because you have written something to be shared. I can't wait to read your fall journal. I think you enjoy writing. It's ok! Your secret is safe with me.

Yours Truly,
Mrs. Magle
A+

P.S. I have a big surprise for you!

CPSIA information can be obtained at www.ICGtesting.com
Printed in the USA
LVOW06s0323300414

383691LV00001B/1/P